FIFTY TO ONE!

Bullets whizzed around Tracker's ears as he sped through the trees zig-zagging from side to side while the killers opened up the accelerators on their four-wheelers and gave chase. He whirled around, quickly reloaded the two Desert Eagles, dropping the expended magazines at his feet. He slapped the forty-fours back into their holsters on his hips and snatched the crossbow off his back. Tracker picked out the ATV that was farthest back, drew and fired. He looked up to see the arrow bounce harmlessly off the man's Kevlar vest. Tracker had miscalculated and not shown Kevlar the respect it deserved. He then looked at his dog Titan and pointed at the nearby treeline. ''Titan, go.''

The big wolf/dog looked at the trees and then at the wave of fifty men coming across the meadow. The beast sat still, ears pricked. Angry, Natty said, ''Titan, go!''

The giant wolf/dog growled. Tracker snapped. ''Fine, stay and get killed, you flea-ridden sonofa-bitch.'' Tracker sighted the gauge on the oncoming vehicles and switched the lever to HE for high explosive and fired . . .

The TRACKER series by Ron Stillman

TRACKER
DEATH HUNT

RON STILLMAN

DIAMOND BOOKS, NEW YORK

DEATH HUNT

A Diamond Book / published by arrangement with
the author

PRINTING HISTORY
Diamond edition / November 1991

ISBN: 1-55773-632-4

Diamond Books are published by The Berkley Publishing
Group, 200 Madison Avenue, New York, New York 10016.
The name "DIAMOND" and its logo are trademarks
belonging to Charter Communications, Inc.

PRINTED IN THE UNITED STATES OF AMERICA

10 9 8 7 6 5 4 3 2 1

To Shirley
You're the *real* "love muffin"
This one's for you.
Love,
The *real* Ron Stillman

DEATH HUNT

1.

The Bowhunter

SARA LYNN BROCKMAN grew up in the country on a small farm in the Oil City area of Pennsylvania. She loved the farmlands around her home, and she often went out with her dad to plant corn, work the farm, or sometimes just to watch him shoot woodchucks. The varmints were plentiful in the Seven Mountains area and they dug holes all over her daddy's fields.

They would walk out from the house and head into one of the surrounding patches of woods. Her dad carried a bolt action .243 Remington with a leather sling and a variable three- to nine-power scope on it. She got to carry the two small leather-covered sandbags. Her dad would set the two sandbags down on top of each other on a stump at the edge of a large field, and then rest the stock of his flat-shooting rifle on top of them. Picking out a woodchuck way out in the farm field, he then took aim and fired. The groundhogs often stood on their hindlegs to look around for danger with their sharp vision. That is when the little girl's dad shot.

After he fired, the other woodchucks all scurried for their holes and didn't come back out for fifteen minutes to a half hour. During that time, her father lit his pipe and talked to her about the earth and its people. Sara Lynn was entranced by the words and the wisdom of her daddy. To her, he was the smartest, most wonderful person in the whole world.

They sometimes rode into town together to buy groceries for her mom or seed for the farm. Many of their neighbors were Amish and Mennonite, and she noticed that a lot of the other farmers never spoke to the strange black-garbed people with their black horse-drawn buggies. It was not that way with her father, however; the Amish seemed to like him, and he often stopped to carry on a conversation with some bearded Amish farmer. They were men of the soil and seemed to respect her dad, who showed them respect as well.

It was during these times in her childhood that Sara Lynn developed such a deep and abiding love of the outdoors. That is why she, a gorgeous and intelligent television news anchorwoman with a major network station in New York, was wearing Trebark camouflage and looking down from her tree stand in the Adirondacks watching for a monstrous-sized whitetail buck deer.

Sara Lynn had an hourglass figure, beautiful brown hair, and almond-colored eyes that were wide, bright, and intelligent. This was now covered with Trebark camouflage coveralls and a camouflage headnet. In her hand was a Jennings compound bow set at sixty pounds with a fifty percent let-off at half-pull. It also had a screw-in bow quiver with Easton XX75 Gamegetter arrows topped by screw-in, four-bladed, Barrie Rocky Mountain broad razor hunting heads.

Sara had taken a forkhorn buck when she was sixteen years old in the woods behind their farm with her dad watching and telling her what to do. He not only had developed in the young girl a love for hunting but an appreciation for nature and taught her to be a conservationist as well. She didn't believe in killing game just for the sake of killing, nor did she believe in wasting meat or taking game from a diminished population area.

Her dad taught her, for example, that animals such as deer, if not taken by controlled harvest, remained within one mile of where they were born, no matter how hard pressed. If too many deer were allowed to live in a certain area, they would over populate and either die by spreading brainworms or the browse line on trees and bushes would keep getting higher and higher. So in the dead of winter, only the tallest deer, standing on their hindlegs, got food. The rest of the deer starved to death, because it was not instinctive for them to move away from their home area.

Sara Lynn and her husband, a nationally famous night-club comedian and a devoted duck and pheasant hunter, would watch television in their Manhattan penthouse and laugh as they listened to the very vocal animal right activists talk about going into the woods and banging pans on the opening day of hunting season to scare away all the deer. Like other experienced hunters, they knew how ridiculous that statement was, and they questioned how many times these kooks had ever been in the woods and how much they truly appreciated nature.

The male whitetail deer, especially a mature buck, goes through some incredible changes during the onset of the "rut," which occurs during the fall. The rut is mating season, and mature bucks, which are normally very wary and careful, become like others of their gender in many species. In other words, they become horny males. A mature buck will select an oblong territory that is normally about two to six miles long and from fifty yards to one and a half-mile wide. During the rut, nose to the ground like an old coon dog, the buck will constantly traverse the perimeter of this territory to smell for does in estrus that he could breed with or for challenging bucks entering his territory and wanting to take over his harem.

Every once in a while, the buck will create a scrape,

which is a spot on the ground where he paws away all the brush, stones, leaves, and grass. The scrape can be anywhere from one foot in diameter to four feet, and is dependent on the size of the buck that makes it. After pawing the ground away the buck then stands in the center of it with all four hooves together and his back hunched up. He then urinates down the inside of his hindlegs, and the urine travels across two musk-filled scent glands just above the inside of his hind knees. This scent runs down the legs and into the dirt in the scrape. He then stands on his hindlegs and chews an overhanging branch and rubs forehead scent on it.

This signpost lets interested females know who he is and where they should come for some "good loving." It is thought that placing a scrape where the buck could stand on his hindlegs and chew the overhead branch intimidates any other smaller bucks who want to enter the territory to steal does. If a doe in estrus enters the territory, she also hunches her back up, with feet together, and urinates into the scrape. Another sign of the buck during the rut is that his neck swells up from the effects of an excess of testosterone.

Many good deer hunters are called scrape hunters, because they put a tree stand overlooking one of these scrapes, knowing that the buck will eventually come by, checking for does in heat. Sara Lynn was doing that very thing.

She heard a noise that sounded like a large dog huffing and puffing along, and suddenly a massive fourteen-point buck appeared sniffing the ground and heading for his scrape. Her heart pounded but she calmed herself down. Knowing that deer seldom look up for danger, she felt that she was reasonably safe from being spotted on her portable tree stand. She moved slowly and raised her bow. An arrow was already nocked, so she held it between her index and middle finger and got ready to draw the string back with three fingers.

The buck moved into the scrape and turned sideways. She took a breath and drew back the arrow and held it at her anchor point. Sara Lynn aimed a little low and behind the left shoulder and concentrated. Her mouth was closed, and she breathed through her nose. She took another breath and then let it halfway out. Sara let the string slip off the tips of her three fingers and the arrow shot out of the bow. The mighty buck tried to jump at the sound of the bow, but he was too late. The arrow buried itself all the way up to the fletchings right behind the left shoulder. It penetrated the lung, sliced off a rib, and cut through the heart. The big stag bolted away into the forest.

Sara Lynn noticed that she was perspiring heavily and panting so hard that she was hyperventilating. Her legs felt rubbery, and she sat down hard on her tree stand. Arms and hands trembling, she grabbed the tree for support. She had to urinate very badly, so she climbed down, dropped her drawers and peed below the stand. Then she started laughing and almost clapped her hands.

She calmed herself down again and spoke out loud to herself, "Nice shot, Ms. Brockman. Now calm down and sit down and wait about fifteen minutes. If you follow him right away, his adrenaline will keep pumping and he'll keep going. The buck will suffer, and you might not find him. Let him lay down and he'll stiffen, go to sleep, and simply die."

Finishing up relieving her kidneys, she reached into her hip pocket for a tissue when a voice came from behind her, "Don't bother pulling the clothes back on. Pull the rest of them all the way off."

She turned and three men were standing there with shotguns in their hands. All three were laughing and staring at her lustfully. Sara Lynn started crying as she pulled her clothes off. She could tell they meant business.

While two held guns on her, each took his turn raping her, biting her, and forcing her to fellate him. She begged and pleaded, but each time she spoke, she was slapped or punched. Afterward, they stood over the naked terrified woman and laughed at her.

"Why are you doing this to me?" she cried.

The leader said, "Because our organization is going to rid the world of all the assholes like you that want to kill all the animals, send our boys off to wars to be killed, and kill the rest of us with nuclear fallout and holes in the ozone layer."

"What are you talking about? You're crazy!" she cried.

He spoke again, "No, we're just doing what somebody has finally got to do to get the madness to stop, and unfortunately, lady, you're going to be one of the examples."

He fired both barrels of his twelve gauge shotgun, and she died instantly.

Harvey Billups had been a game warden with the New York State Division of Wildlife for twenty-one years and had never seen anything like it. He waited for the homicide detectives and the coroner's office before he even touched the buck's carcass. The lab people cut the deer down from the high branch. They cut the leather stitches along the belly of the hollowed-out carcass and grabbed the nude woman's body. Her blood was mixed with that of the deer into which she had been laced.

Harvey just stared and said, "Son of a fucking bitch."

2.

The Environmentalist

THE BRAVE MOVED forward ten slow steps. He froze in place, then slowly knelt and looked all around under the low hanging branches of the pinions and cedars. The brave listened but only heard the far-off cry of a red-tailed hawk. Moving along quietly, he wore only soft-soled moccasins, a breechcloth, Bowie-sized knife in beaded sheath, and a single eagle feather in his hair.

His big buckskin gelding, named Eagle, followed about ten feet behind him. Unlike the normal Indian pony, descended from Spanish Barbs, it was a sixteen-hand-high, barrel-chested, full-blooded quarter horse.

The brave himself, however, was not a full blood, but a mixed breed. He had one grandparent who was from the plains tribe, the Assiniboin Lakotah, or Sioux, and another grandparent from the Tonto Apache tribe in the Southwest. The other two grandparents were what influenced his unusual and unique appearance. One was a blond-haired, blue-eyed Norwegian, while the other was a tall black woman from Kenya. Consequently, the brave had wavy black hair, dark copper skin, and light powder-blue eyes that were the color of the summer sky in the Southwest.

Having pushed himself much harder than those about him for all of his thirty-some years, the brave was built like the ideal candidate to star in a Tarzan movie. Handsome as a leading man, he stood six feet four with a narrow waist, washboard stomach, broad shoulders, and an overdeveloped chest and upper arms. His legs were long and muscled with what seemed like a series of steel cables and pulleys.

He had numerous scars on his magnificent body from previous battles, including two half-moon bite scars that covered his entire right calf muscle area. There were spear wounds through the left shoulder muscle and the lower right abdomen, near the appendix area. A bit above that, there was a stab wound that had punctured a lung. The left thigh had a scar from a bullet that had come through the muscle from behind. It was obvious that this man was a warrior, and more importantly, one who didn't lose in battle.

What was more impressive than anything else though, were the man's eyes. Set above the high cheekbones, the powder-blue eyes showed great wisdom and a constant confident smile. This warrior was obviously a man who was always on top of whatever life threw at him. This quiet confidence was what made his enemies fear and respect him and made the most independent women dream about being softly held in his protective arms.

Clutching a handmade seventy pound-pull lemonwood bow in his left hand, he stopped and froze again after ten more steps. His powerful eyes scanned the ground below him and looked at the tracks and signs of the large buck the brave had been tracking. The V-shaped tracks were large and deep which could simply indicate a very big doe; however, this particular brave was the very best there was at tracking. He spotted the tiny groove along the side of the round manure pellets excreted by the mule deer. The pellets of the doe were completely round while the bucks always produced a small groove along one side because of a growth in the anal tube. He was so knowledgeable about tracking, in fact, that his Sioux name translated to "He Who Tracks the Eagle" and his Apache name translated to "He Who Tracks."

The tracks indicated that the deer was still moving slowly and wasn't spooked. The brave's horse wore leather boots over his shod hooves and knew not to whinny or make noise. It, too, bore scars on its muscled body and was indeed a war horse. He simply followed along very slowly, occasionally cropping grass, while his master worked out the trail. The brave tossed up some dry weed tops in the air and made sure the wind was still blowing across from his left to his right.

He knew that the buck would soon make his bed for the afternoon, probably at the head of a brushy draw. The brave would then leave the horse and make his final stalk after the old stag. He had singled out this deer, as he only needed one deer for meat right now, and the older buck would be replaced by one of many younger challengers.

The white man could learn some valuable lessons about animal husbandry, wildlife conservation, reforestation, and environmental protection from the American Indian. The Indians took only the animals that were needed for food and used the rest of the carcass for clothing, shelter, tools, and glue. They knew that without the land, their tribes would perish, so the Native Americans never tried to kill animals needlessly, but only for life-giving reasons. Some of the more primitive ways of taking bison, such as panicking a herd and driving them over a cliff were somewhat wasteful, but as the weapons of the Indians improved, so did their methods for taking game.

The brave spotted a movement ahead of him and froze with one foot raised. It was the buck, a six-by-six, with twelve long antler tines sticking up from a wide-spread trunk thicker than his forearm. It was grazing on some buckbrush about fifty feet ahead. It was right along the edge of the summit of a downhill slope that was dotted with small gnarled pinions and covered with sand and rock. The warrior turned and gave his horse, Eagle, a look that the big horse immediately understood. The mighty steed stood there, ears pricked forward, nostrils flaring in and out, trying to pick up a scent on the breeze. He spotted the buck and froze, too.

Branches between the hunter and quarry were too low for a clear shot, so he started moving forward very slowly. He licked his lips and felt the coolness on one side, reassuring himself that the wind was still blowing crosswise. The warrior set one foot down in extreme slow motion, followed by the other. He watched the buck while he felt the twigs, stones, and ground beneath his feet through the soft-soled moccasins. If he felt a twig, he simply stopped his foot, then raised it slowly and set it down elsewhere. The brave knew that deer are incapable of seeing stationary objects and are also incapable of seeing anything but the ground beneath them when their heads are down grazing, so he kept his eyes focused on the buck's tail. Deer have a nerve that connects between the head and the base of the tail, so when a grazing deer with its head down is going to lift its head up, look around, smell, listen, and then graze again, it slightly twitches the tail a split-second before raising its head. Knowing this, the brave kept his eyes on the tail, and when it moved, he froze until the head went down again.

The warrior also followed the old Indian habit of not staring at his quarry, so the animal didn't sense a predator and get spooked. Doing this, the brave kept moving closer and closer, but branches still were in the way of a clear shot, and the wise warrior never took a chancy shot with a bow. He had killed and wounded others in battle but had no desire to needlessly wound an animal, letting it go off to suffer in pain and maybe die much later. Like other Indian hunters, he had picked out the particular animal he was after and tried to communicate with the creature telepathically, letting it know he would not waste any of it, and that he would make a clean kill.

The brave got so close to the two-hundred-pound buck that he squinted when the deer raised its head, so that the shine of his eyeballs wouldn't spook the beast. Unfortunately, the deer had grazed right behind a large cedar tree with branches spreading out in every direction. He finally found an opening big enough for a safe shot behind the big buck's left shoulder and he slowly raised the bow and started to draw back a hand-hewn Port Orford Cedar arrow with turkey feather fletchings and a hand-chipped flint arrowhead.

Suddenly, a tan form silently launched itself from a broad overhanging branch on the far side of the tree and landed squarely on the back of the deer. It was a large tom mountain lion, and it quickly bit into the spine of the deer on the back of its neck. The deer kicked and squirmed a few times, but the powerful jaws of the hunter severed the animal's spine, and the warrior, arrow drawn, knew the mighty buck was in its death throes.

The brave had an easy shot at the cougar, which was now making sure the deer was going to stop moving, but the warrior smiled and lowered his bow. He watched as the deer stopped moving and the big cat immediately bit into the belly of the fresh carcass. The brave took a slow cautionary step backward, and the big cat whirled, blood dripping off its whiskered jaws. It growled, ready to defend its kill.

The brave spoke softly, "Brother Cat, I do not seek your meal. You must try many times to kill one deer, but I will find another. I ate yesterday, but you have but old dreams in your belly. I walk back to my horse and will leave you in peace, for I do not stalk the great cat this day."

While the big cat growled and hissed, ears flattened on his round head, the mighty brave slowly backed away. After thirty paces he turned and walked briskly toward his big dun horse. There was little chance that the shy mountain cat would try an attack. Cougars like easy kills and are normally deathly afraid of humans and dogs. Even small dogs have been known to tree full-grown cougars.

Returning to the horse, the brave swung up on the muscular back and skirted a large mountain meadow as he headed west toward the majestic snow-capped Sangre de Cristo range, fifteen miles distant. Named by early Spanish explorers because of their red hue in both the rising and setting sun, the name means "Blood of Christ." The range is considered by many to be the most pristine and beautiful in all of the Rockies.

Out of earshot of the lion, not wanting to disturb it any more than he already had, the brave gave a long whistle. After two minutes, a large gray, white, and black beast appeared at the warrior's side. Weighing over two hundred pounds of muscle and scar tissue, it was half timberwolf and half Malamute. The wolf/dog had blood on his chops, which he licked. He looked up at his master and wagged his tail as he trotted proudly next to the raw-boned horse.

They trotted steadily toward a lesser peak than those of the Sangre de Cristo. The very rocky, boulder-strewn peak was called Lookout Mountain due to its use by the Cheyenne and the Utes when they used this area for their winter hunting grounds. Later outlaws who robbed trains traveling the nearby Arkansas River Canyon between Salida and Canon City, Colorado, used the mountain for the same purpose.

Rounding a bend in the trail, the brave came face to face with ten armed men on all-terrain vehicles. Each wore a motorcycle helmet, Kevlar bullet-proof vest, and black coveralls. They carried MAC-10 automatic machine pistols, AK-47 assault rifles, and Uzis. Each wore a black web ammo belt with hand grenades and additional magazines as well as holsters with pistols.

All of a sudden, the brave heard many more ATVs starting up and even more vehicles started coming at him from all directions. He didn't even consider these, he had no choice; he could only worry about the ten immediately in front of him.

He thought in a millisecond about the odds. The brave was on a horse and had a primitive bow and about ten handmade arrows in a quiver. He had a Bowie knife on his hip and a fighting wolf/dog at his side. His enemies, counting those coming but still out of sight, numbered maybe fifty. All had automatic weapons, plus backup guns, body armor, and gas-powered all-terrain vehicles.

He did have several things in his favor, however: he had surprised the ambushers as much as they surprised him; he had a brain that was superior to most with whom he came in contact; he was very experienced at fighting. Most important, however, was the fact that he was Nathaniel Hawthorne Tracker, America's number one human weapon. He was a former U.S. Air Force major who piloted F-15 Eagle fighter jets, a black belt in Tae Kwon Do and accomplished in judo, jujitsu, aikido, and ninjitsu. A genius with computers and radar, he had numerous patents to his name, and his body alone was a miracle of science. This was a man who had saved the President of the United States from an assassin. He had rid the world of a number of major terrorists and dismantled several criminal organizations and empires. Tracker was a one-man army now facing another army of assassins, but since they had researched whom they were up against, they had brought a change of clothes and plenty of reinforcements.

Two men took arrows between the body armor and the helmet before anybody could unsling his weapon, aim, and get off a shot. Another had his windpipe ripped out by a two-hundred-pound beast that hit him with a leap. The rest fired several hundred bullets at thin, mountain air, as the horse, man, and wolf/dog jumped over the heads of the two closest killers and dove over the brink of a precipice and ran almost straight downhill for four hundred feet, disappearing into the thick forest below.

Hitting the bottom of the slope, Tracker pushed Eagle into a full gallop, dodging in and out of trees toward a narrow steep-sided gulch. Plunging into the gulch, man and horse broke through a flock of almost one hundred wild turkeys and followed a narrow game trail downhill at a slow angle, knowing pursuit would be not far behind. Tracker reached up and pushed the skin behind and under his right ear, and a sensor activated videorecorders and monitors in the computer center of his mansion in Colorado Springs and some in the Washington, D.C. office of Undersecretary of State Wally Rampart. The retired general seated behind his desk looked up at the view of a wild gulch rushing forward at a dizzying pace. He reached up under his desk and pushed a red button. Tracker immediately felt three slight electrical pulses in his right leg at the base of his kneecap.

Dodging trees, rocks, and fallen logs, Tracker said, "General, I'm without weapons and ran into about fifty hitmen in Kevlar and riding ATVs. All are wearing matching helmets, black coveralls, and carrying automatic weapons and so on. I'm heading for that new hideout we installed on my mountain property for times like this. I'll let you know if I need help, but I'm pissed and want to teach these jerks a lesson. Got that? No reinforcements unless I ask for them."

He felt three electric pulses in his right knee and grinned just as the big horse broke out into a much wider gulch and galloped across it and up an old mining road. He turned into a stand of pine trees and reined the horse, who did a perfectly square sliding stop.

Natty Tracker told the horse and wolf/dog, Titan, to stand where they were. He ran over and grabbed a tree branch, twisted it, and suddenly, a ten-by-ten-feet square of ground under the two animals started moving downwards like a giant freight elevator. He ran over and jumped down next to the horse and dog and was literally swallowed by the ground. Thirty seconds later, the missing patch of ground rose back up through the concrete walls and locked into position where it had been before. The seams for the giant trap door were undetectable and the branch that Natty had twisted as well as the whole tree could be viewed from scant inches, and it could not be determined that it was all made of vinyl and plastic.

The next few minutes found two dozen all-terrain vehicles roaring around, over, and past the underground hiding place.. Not one of the riders had any clue as to what was there. In the meantime, underground, Natty Tracker was preparing for battle.

The twenty-four-hundred acre parcel of mountain property that Natty owned was at just under eight thousand feet on the eastern side of the Wet Mountain Valley in an area referred to by locals as the Deer Mountain area or Glen Vista, after a subdivision there. Thirty miles southwest of Canon City and sixteen miles northeast of Westcliffe, it was only accessible by two hard-packed dirt roads called Copper Gulch Road and Road Gulch Road. The entire property was completely fenced in, and Natty often went there to get away from it all. He kept several head of horses there that watered at a set of natural springs called Ross Springs and grazed on acres of mountain grasses.

There was a problem in the area with loco weed, but Tracker had found out what chemicals to use from the U.S. Soil Conservation Service and sprayed the meadows annually. The horses only had to be moved for one week each year while the loco was being killed and then could return. Loco weed is the first graze that ripens in the springtime and many horses, cattle, and wildlife will graze on it. During that one-week period the animals actually get stoned and will sometimes buck or shy from their owners. Some of those animals, especially horses, will actually become addicted to the weed with its purple or white blossoming tops. The weed affects their brain and liver, eventually destroying both. The animal continues to feed on the loco weed, with it becoming more and more important to their diet each day, until they reach the point that they only eat loco weed and finally give up even drinking water. The animals, at that point, become totally disoriented and crash through five-strand barbed wire fences, run into tree branches and are reduced to skin and bones. They have tremors throughout their muscles, and if you move your hand or anything near their heads, they will throw themselves over backward.

Even at eight thousand feet, the southern Colorado winters were relatively mild and didn't get that much snow. When there was a heavy snowfall, Natty had a local rancher put out grass and alfalfa for his horses. There were also several barns and lean-to shelters on the property where the horses could go during storms. Along with the horses, deer and elk occasionally grazed, and a small herd of pronghorns was almost always on the property from around May until September, when they rejoined the larger herds outside Westcliffe and Silver Cliff.

Tracker briefly had a one-hundred-million-dollar bounty on his head by a group that included Saddam Hussein and Muhammar Qadhafi. Prior to that, Wacky Kadaffy had put a ten-million-dollar bounty on his head because Natty had infiltrated Tripoli, Libya. Not once but twice, he had been put into prison in Libya and tortured by a notorious Cuban terrorist called The Ratel. Although The Ratel had amputated Tracker's left ring finger and raped and sodomized the woman Tracker loved in front of him, Natty was able to escape after he and his lover, Doctor Fancy Bird, had captured and killed The Ratel. She was then killed in Tripoli harbor by another Cuban mercenary who Natty also eventually killed. After Tracker infiltrated Iraq with his "sterilized" F-15E Eagle jet and dropped the body of a famous Iraqi hitman through the roof of So-Damn Insane's palace, Hussein and Qadhafi had decided their money could be better spent than wasting it on a bounty on a harmless infidel.

Because of the bounties, though, along with attempts by other criminal organizations to eliminate Tracker, his 2,400 acre getaway in the mountains had become a very dangerous territory for him to visit. Tracker's beautiful mansion in the Broadmoor area of Colorado Springs at the base of Cheyenne Mountain and NORAD headquarters had been breached several times by different would-be assassins, but Natty had improved his home's security system after each incident. Since he had improved the security there, it was much easier to come after him at his mountain property. Especially since he, oft times, outfitted himself only in the traditional dress and weapons of his red ancestors.

After the last attempt at killing him on the mountain property, Natty, a multi-millionaire because of his many important patents, had installed his underground hideaway where he was now preparing a cup of coffee and a steak sandwich. He figured that if he was going to battle fifty armed killers, he ought to, at least, have some food in his stomach. He gave Titan several pounds of prime meat and grained and watered Eagle, after a rubdown and a cooldown period while Natty ate lunch.

His underground bunker was air-conditioned, humidified, and had about two thousand square feet of floor space. There was a computer, FAX, phone, monitors, sleeping area, weapons room, a stall for Eagle, bathroom, a parking area for one of his inventions called the Hovercopter, and a kitchen. Looking at the Sony Trintron screen on his bunker wall, Tracker had a video view of his government contact, retired Army Brigadier General Wally Rampart, a special Undersecretary of State who reported directly to the President of the United States. The two carried on a humorous conversation while Natty prepared his meal, fed his animals, changed clothes, and selected his weapons for battle.

"You sure you don't want help?" Wally asked.

"Of course," Natty said sarcastically, "I've always been kind of indecisive, and now that I think about it, this rag-tag army of badasses scares the crap out of me, so please send in the army and air force."

Tracker laughed while Wally said, "Okay, fuck you, smartass."

Tracker worked for the government as an independent contractor/private investigator on tough cases that would embarrass the government if they were blown or publicized, especially if they were carried out by an actual government employee. Wally Rampart acted as a buffer between the President and Tracker in case of discovery. At first, he worried about the chances that Natty took. In fact, he often acted like a mother hen, but Tracker had let him know that he was his own boss. More importantly, Tracker had become a legend in the intelligence and law enforcement business with some of his incredible feats and exploits. If Natty thought he could tackle fifty armed killers, Wally would just keep certain military types standing by at nearby Fort Carson and Petersen Air Force Base, but he didn't bother Tracker with the details.

Besides his training, intelligence, cunning, ferociousness in battle, and great strength, Tracker was probably the most dangerous warrior in the world because of his incredible inventions.

Blinded in a car wreck while in the Air Force in Alaska, Tracker first developed the SOD System, an acronym for Sonar Optic Device. He learned how to function without sight by wearing a hearing device that sent beeps to his ear from a microchip. This chip sent out and received sonar waves and then translated them into deep beeps for large objects and high tones for small ones. These beeps were closer together if the object was close and farther apart when it was at a distance.

After that, working with opthamologists and scientists, Tracker developed the OPTIC System, an acronym for Optical Initiation Contrivance. This was a set of specially made glasses that functioned as a pair of high-tech video cameras. The frames had two outlets with detachable fiber optic filaments that emerged from Natty's eyebrows. These filaments were attached to fiber optic mesh screens installed by laser surgery in Natty's optic nerves. Whatever the lenses focused on stimulated the optic nerves in a dot matrix pattern like a video camera and enabled Tracker to see in a rudimentary fashion.

Following that, Tracker upgraded the SOD system so the sonar pulses indicated the distance to any object Natty looked at. This compensated for the cameras' lack of depth perception. He also gave the OPTIC System a night vision capability and added a zoom function to it.

Natty then had another operation that replaced the OPTIC System glasses with highly miniaturized video cameras contained in permanent contact lenses in his eyes. The left side of his left eye had a gauge that indicated on a graph how far objects were from him in feet and inches. He could zoom his eyesight in and out by simply squinting his eyes, and he also had a sensor implanted behind and under his right ear which started and stopped video recorders and monitors in his own computer center and in Wally Rampart's office. Whatever Tracker saw was then immediately transmitted to both locations.

The OPTIC System glasses had also been tremendously upgraded by Tracker. Some months before, he had demonstrated their capabilities at Fort Bragg, North Carolina at the Saint Mere Eglise Drop Zone and then at Lee Field House, where he explained the unique invention to the President and other major governmental officials.

Writing on a whiteboard while he spoke, Natty had attempted to put it in layman's terms, saying, "We all look at light every second of every minute of every waking day, day in and day out, week by week, throughout every year of our lives. Light is a visible form of energy. It is made up of colors, primarily red, blue, and green. Not purple, yellow, orange, or any of the other colors you see when you refract light through a prism. That is why you will hear those dealing with television or video talking about the RBG signal. The RBG stands for red, blue, and green. Each color is in itself a form of electromagnetic energy, and each color has a specific wavelength. Stay with me on this, please. Now the energy in colors, the electromagnetic vibrations, are so minute that they must be measured in nanometers. One nanometer is one millionth of a millimeter, and all colors range between 380 nanometers and 720 nanometers. Some colors vibrate faster than others, so when light enters your eye, it hits the back of the eyeball on the retina. Getting to the retina, the light is refracted like a prism so the colors are translated, some farther back in the eye and some closer forward because those with less vibration move through the prism faster, so they hit the back of the eyeball slightly in advance of other colors. Who's still with me?''

The President and about half the others raised their hands. Natty chuckled.

He continued, ''I apologize. I get excited about this and try to explain in too much detail. Okay, also on the back of your eye, you have rods and cones; the cones translate color values and the rods translate light and dark values. All of this incoming information in a wave of light is transferred through the optic nerve to the brain, where it is sorted out. Some of the colors go to a spot in the left brain and others go to a spot in the right brain. Now, the left side of the brain controls our creativity, subconscious, and so on, and the right side controls our logical thinking, ability to reason, etc. When we think, we think in color in our brains.''

The President interrupted, ''Excuse me, Mr. Tracker, this thing about light penetrating the eye and then getting translated into different colors. Are you saying that the eye translates light beams into color like the ear translates sound waves into what we hear?''

Natty grinned, "I know what you're getting at, Mr. President: if the tree falls in the woods, is there a sound, or is there only a sound if someone's there to hear it? I'm afraid it's the same type of argument. Colors are just waves of electromagnetic energy mixed together to form light beams. They enter the eye and are translated into color. Those of you who are hunters may be aware that deer, for example, only see in black and white. That's because they have only rods in the backs of their eyes and not cones. To make a simple example of the strength of the energy in light, everybody knows how much power there is in a laser beam. To simplify it, when you make all the waves of several colors peak and dip simultaneously, in other words, vibrate at exactly the same speed, then you create a laser beam."

Tracker had to pause and take a swallow of water and grinned while looking out at the crowd as several of them scratched their heads.

He looked at the assembled faces, smiled, and turned around to set down the white board and the charts he had been using, then faced about.

Natty went on, "Okay, I'm cutting through all the bull-shit. I can look at a person while I'm wearing the OPTIC System and see an aura of colors around him given off by electromagnetic waves from his brain and body. In a controlled situation, such as here in this gymnasium, if I had a small group with each member sitting separately, I could actually see small color pictures of your thought patterns in an electromagnetic halo around your head. The OPTIC System has been set up with the capability to function as a super-hypersensitive spectrograph, the instrument used to measure the nanometers in waves of color. The more emotional you are, the easier it is to vaguely see the thought pictures. In other words, we still have almost a decade to go to get to the twenty-first century, but the Tracker OPTIC System enables the wearer to physically read a person's mind, or at least see the person's stronger mental pictures. Of course, this will have to be secretly tested, by me, for an extended period of time, but use your imagination, and just think of the possibilities and practical applications of this system.''

Another device in Tracker's body was a miniature, but very powerful, laser system installed in the stump of his amputated left ring finger. Natty could remove the fake finger, push a small button, and the laser mechanism activated. He had used this more than once to save his life, and sometimes, to end others'.

The laser system and the audio/video transmitter and receiver capabilities in Natty's body were powered by a nuclear cell in a hermetically sealed capsule implanted in his shin.

Another of Tracker's inventions was called the Tracker System which was worn on the wrist like a watch. A digital readout, using sonar and infrared capabilities copied from those used by heat-seeking missiles, it gave a digital readout of the distance, speed, and direction of travel of any warm-bodied line-of-sight creature.

Still another invention was the EAR System, an acronym for Enhanced Audio Receiver. The EAR System was a miniature directional microphone and radio receiver. It was funnel-shaped and operated like the dish-shaped directional mikes seen on the sidelines at NFL football games. Tracker could listen to conversations in a building by removing the EAR from a fake rabbit's foot keychain and placing it in his ear and then turning his ear toward a window in the building. It could pick up the conversation by the vibrations on the window pane. He could also listen to people talking from several hundred yards away.

Tracker had a definite love for flight and had been given a present of a brand new ''sterilized'' F-15E Eagle turbothruster fighter jet aircraft. He also had a single-engine Cessna, a helicopter, and had recently been shot down in a twin-engine Beechcraft.

Another invention of Tracker's was the Hovercopter

which he was now readying for use against the fifty-man
army of assassins he was now facing. The Hovercopter
was a cross between a one-man helicopter and a one-man
hovercraft. It looked like a miniature helicopter built on
top of an overturned six-man whitewater raft, and he could
switch from helicopter mode to hovercraft, or vice-versa,
with the simple pull of a lever. It had an M-60 machinegun mounted on the front and it moved from side to side
or up and down commensurate with Natty's head movements while wearing his flight helmet. He also could fire
six-round bursts of 7.62 millimeter bullets by biting down
on a mouth-fired trigger mechanism. He could also fire
four rifle grenades at once, or individually, with a weapon
he developed by welding together the barrels and cham-
bers of four M-79 grenade launchers and adding a trig-
gering device operated by his foot.

Tracker decided to start out as he was already dressed.
He had wreaked havoc on one of the world's richest men
and biggest criminals named James Earl Smith and had
fought and dismantled the neo-Nazi racist organization
called the Aryan Society for Racial Purity dressed in his
Native American garb. He had been labeled "the Phan-
tom" by Smith and was extremely intimidating. It was
also therapeutic and fun for him to vanquish his enemies
like his ancestors had done, so many years before the ad-
vent of cellular phones, crunching Pac-Man monsters, and
Stealth bombers.

Tracker had one thing to add and that was war paint.
He first removed the leather boots from Eagle and then
tied his tail in a knot to indicate he was at war. He then
put red hand prints on each side of the big horse's rump
and painted red stripes around the horse's forelegs. He
also tied eagle feathers into his mount's tail and mane.
Natty then put his own war paint on. He made a black
racoon-eye mask first and then, covering his fingers on
both hands with red paint, he started them at the nose and

made two sets of eagle talons going outward from the center of his face.

Tracker then went over to his computer desk and looked at the bank of security monitors showing scenes from cameras hidden in trees around the property. He grabbed his traditional weapons and mounted Eagle, pushed the button for the elevator and trap door and went out for his second skirmish with the enemy. Natty knew that while he was out facing the killers, Wally would be using all the governmental intelligence and police organizations available to figure out where this group of killers was from and why they were attacking him.

Tracker pushed the sensor behind his ear so Wally could monitor what was going on. He didn't know that quite often, like now, the President was in Wally's office also watching.

Above ground, Tracker headed his buckskin farther up the mining road toward the northeastern end of his property. He rode through a steep-sided gulch with rocky cliffs along the right and tall evergreens on the left. After a quarter of a mile, he passed two old mines on the left side and spooked two large mule deer bucks that appeared over the ridgeline to his left. They were about two hundred yards apart. This let him know that somebody was over in the next gulch searching for him and traveling in the same direction as Natty. He knew from watching the monitors that the killers had split up into groups of five, and one of these groups should be not far ahead of him moving along slowly. He knew that they would spread out shortly when the gulch widened with two gently inclined, wooded ridgelines.

Tracker heard the low sound of the ATVs slowly moving ahead of him around a bend in the gully. He remained patient and kept the same pace. Five minutes later, they were in sight. He squeezed Eagle's flanks with his calves and the big horse stepped out a little faster, knowing that they were stalking the prey ahead. Natty picked out the

ATV that was the farthest back, and he went forward at a fast walk which was faster than the trot of many horses. Natty drew an arrow back and fired, aiming at the middle of the man's back. He started nocking another arrow immediately, but looked up to see the first arrow make the man bend forward in pain, but it bounced harmlessly off the Kevlar vest. He heard the man's yelp of pain, as did the others.

Tracker had miscalculated and had not shown Kevlar the respect it deserved. He fired the second arrow at the first man to bring his gun to bear. Natty saw the arrow streaking toward the killer's face as he wheeled his horse into a roll-back. A roll-back is a maneuver in which the horseman skids the horse to a sliding stop, then pulls up and to the side on the reins at the same time that he pushes into the ribs with the heel on the same side he reins toward. At the same time, he applies a knee aid, or knee pressure, on the opposite shoulder. A well-trained horse will slide to a stop, rear up, and at the same time, twist its body backward in the direction he's being reined, and take off in the direction he had just come from. The horse actually is rolling back over its hips. In the case of Eagle, he could come to a dead stop on a dime, do a roll-back, and leave nine cents change.

Bullets whizzed around Tracker's ears as he sped through the trees zig-zagging the horse from side to side while the killers opened up the accelerators on their four-wheelers and gave chase. Natty glanced at a small ridge off to his left and quickly reined Eagle in that direction. He smiled as he remembered what was right at the top of the wooded ridge. They made it to the top and the big horse slid to a halt, sides heaving. In front of him was an old earthquake split in the hard ground. The ground just dropped away for about twenty feet, and it was about ten feet across.

Natty spun the big buckskin around, went back down the ridge, did another roll-back, and sprinted back up the hill. The ATVs came into sight as the big horse bolted back up the easy hill. Then, reaching the drop-off, he leapt out into space and landed easily in a dead run on the far side. Tracker went up the next ridgeline, reined in at the top, and watched for the killers. They saw him on the far ridge and roared up the hill. Going up the hill took both of their hands, and he was a far shot anyway, so Natty quickly jumped off his horse, dropped his breechcloth, turned, and mooned the pursuing killers. Enraged and distracted by this act, they saw the twenty foot drop-off too late, and all four ATVs plunged into the ravine screaming. The fifth apparently had indeed taken Natty's arrow through the face. Tracker relieved his bladder, replaced his breechcloth and remounted. He knew more killers would show up, having heard the shots. Tracker disappeared over the ridgeline.

Back in the underground bunker, Tracker's face turned beet red as he looked at Wally Rampart on the big Trinitron screen. The retired general was laughing his head off.

Wally couldn't resist it and finally said, "Some people are geniuses and can even figure out a scientific way to read someone's mind, but they're so fucking dumb they try to penetrate bullet-proof vests with arrows."

Wally laughed hysterically, holding his sides. Fortunately for him, Tracker couldn't reach through the screen and grab his throat right then. Of course, even if Natty had really wanted to kill the older man, a ridiculous thought in itself, Rampart wasn't the type of man who killed easily.

As the late Louis L'Amour used to say, "He had been over the mountain and down the river a time or two."

Wally Rampart was bald, built like a twenty-five-year-old nose tackle for the Bears, and was a consummate worrier. He was loyal to a fault, both up and down the line, and knew how to kiss some ass when he had to. He was just the type of guy who was very selective about the asses that he chose to kiss. Wally had many friends in high places and was also respected by all who knew him, including . . . no, especially his enemies. His nickname, behind his back, was "the walrus" because of his large brown moustache. With that and his size, Wally looked like a cross between a large tough walrus and the actor Wilford Brimley. Consequently, Wally had proved to be one of the most valuable "cornermen" that Natty could have wished for in D.C.

One of the stories that went around Capitol Hill about Undersecretary Rampart was the tale about one of his exploits as a battalion commander with the 82nd Airborne at Fort Bragg, North Carolina. Jumping with his troops over Normandy Drop Zone at Bragg, he had found himself on a C-130 Hercules with one of his young riflemen, a PFC from Augusta, Georgia named Gary Collins. Halfway down his "stick" while jumping out the starboard door of the C-130, Private Collins on his "cherry" jump, exited the door of the aircraft with a vigorous leap out into the prop wash. However, Collins had a very weak body position, his elbows out and eyes closed tight. The turbulent thrust from the powerful prop blast wrapped him and his static line around the tangled collection of spent static lines spinning and thrashing up against the camouflaged skin of the large plane. He was stuck, unconscious, against the tail section of the large aircraft.

SFC King Morgan from Harlem stood in the doorway of the plane looking out at the young trooper. Sergeant Morgan watched, rigger knife in hand, for some sign of consciousness from Private Collins. If Collins were conscious, he was supposed to put his hand on top of his helmet, and Morgan would cut the line, letting Collins fall away safely so he could open up the reserve parachute on his abdomen. Unfortunately, Private Collins simply beat against the craft like a limp rag doll and Sergeant Morgan didn't know what to do.

That's when then-Lieutenant Colonel Wally Rampart took over. Grabbing the rigger's knife from a protesting

Sergeant Morgan, Wally quickly grabbed his own fifteen-foot static line and tied it into a slip knot in his own parachute harness. Then, holding the knife between his teeth, he crawled hand over hand down his own static line. Banging viciously against the plane himself, he cut the bird's nest of twisted static lines away from the limp soldier. Then, wrapping his arms and legs tightly around the unconscious young paratrooper, he reached up and yanked the slip knot out of his own static line. His parachute opened smoothly and he held his young charge all the way down to the sandy drop zone.

The one thing that was different about this particular story on Capitol Hill was that it was totally true. Wally had received the Soldier's Medal for his actions which looked very good with his three Purple Hearts, two Silver Stars, Four Bronze Stars, and the other goodies Wally collected over his illustrious career. As a captain and a company commander with the 173rd Airborne in South Vietnam, Wally was the type of commander that Hollywood screenwriters liked to pattern their heroes after. He was a no-nonsense officer when it came to two things: accomplishing his mission and taking care of his men.

Tracker had actually become like a son to Wally, and he always did almost everything perfectly. So when Tracker did screw up, Wally loved to harass the handsome perfectionist about it. Natty did have an ego. That's one of the reasons he was who he was. On top of that, he really was the consummate perfectionist, so when he erred like he did in forgetting that the assassins were wearing Kevlar vests, it just grated on him to no end.

Cooling down finally, Tracker started grinning, as he walked Eagle onto an electronic treadmill and turned it on slow to cool the horse down. He went to the sink and removed his warpaint while he and Wally talked.

Natty said, "I think this time you said too much General. I'm going to have to prove to you that I can put arrows through guys wearing Kevlar."

Wally lit a big cigar and said, "What the hell're you talking about, Tracker?"

Natty changed clothes, donning a camouflage jumpsuit with pockets all over it and Velcro strips here and there. He started adding holsters, devices, and such to the Velcro strips.

Tracker then picked up a twenty-first century-looking crossbow and said, "Remember when I was working on the new OPTIC System when we tackled the Firefly?"

"Yeah, what about it?"

Natty said, "Well, Pat Madden, the news anchor on the NBC TV affiliate in Colorado Springs and Pueblo was doing an interview with an author who was an ex-Green Beret captain named Don Chase. I had met Chase in Washington one time."

Wally interrupted, "Yeah, I've heard about him. Works trying to help Montagnards from Vietnam. Guy Gray— you've met him, the writer who used to cover all the wars for *Soldier of Fortune*—he works with the Montagnards, too."

Tracker replied, "Yeah, I know. Anyway, Chase is the senior advisor to the President of the Montagnards, and he wrote a book about the discrimination against them by the Vietnamese. The book was called *Crossbow*; you need to read it. Well, when I heard the news story, it started something in my mind going, but I couldn't figure out what. Then a few weeks ago, it hit me. I wanted to develop a new weapon that could be used silently and effectively but faster than a bow or blowgun."

Wally said, "What about a gun and silencer?"

Tracker said, "You can't go any larger than a twenty-two magnum or the silencer isn't effective. Anyway, I came up with this, the Tracker electronic crossbow."

"Electronic crossbow?" Wally responded. "Give me a break, Natty. An electronic crossbow?"

Natty said, "Got all types of heads for it. Just wait, the Army will be begging me for this little darling."

Tracker explained the workings while he showed it to the video camera, "See, the bolts—crossbow arrows—are eighteen inches long and are kept inside three different magazine compartments inside the high-impact polymer stock. There are three different heads: five bolts have heat-seeking devices like missiles, ten bolts have high-explosive heads and shafts, like a small grenade, and fifteen are like normal graphite arrows. When I fire this, the steel bow fires the bolts with the equivalent thrust of a bow with a five hundred pound pull. Two levers that stay attached to the steel cable automatically recock the bow in less than a half a second, and it fires again and again as long as I hold down the trigger. I can actually fire at a rate of one almost every half second."

Wally said, "I'm anxious to see how it works. Good luck."

Tracker replied, "Thanks. I'm going to shut down right now and get my shit together before I go back out."

Wally, a warrior himself, understood and replied, "Roger, 'Luck, Tracker."

General Rampart reached down and shut off the camera and monitor.

Tracker laid down and thought back to the time that he was healing from the shark attack brought on by the orders of James Earl Smith. Natty had brought his Sioux grandfather in from North Dakota to counsel with him before he went after the billionaire criminal.

They had camped in almost the exact spot where Natty had run into the cougar earlier that day. He closed his eyes and smiled as he remembered his grandfather's words.

That night, the two warriors had sat by a small fire and talked about the great hunts of their ancestors. The older spoke of Tracker's relatives who fought in the great battle of the Greasy Grass. That was better known to most of the world as the Battle of the Little Big Horn, or Custer's Last Stand.

His grandfather had told Natty that, according to *his*

grandfather and great uncles who fought there, George Armstrong Custer was actually the fourth one shot. He explained that Custer, while charging across Medicine Tail Coulee, was shot right in the middle of the chest and knocked backward off of his great chestnut thoroughbred named Dandy. Some soldiers picked him out of the water and carried him up the hill, where the whole command was quickly wiped out.

According to his grandfather, Custer, shortly after arriving on the hilltop, shot himself through the right temple with one of his pearl-handled revolvers. That was why the hated officer's body was not stripped, scalped, or touched by any Sioux or Cheyenne, because suicide was so disgraceful among the warriors. Tracker believed the account.

On another night, they had talked about James Earl Smith and the blight he was, not only on the American free enterprise system, but on mankind as well. The younger spoke of his anger and the hate that welled inside him.

The grandfather had said, "My son, iron flows through the blood of the great cat. A wolf lives in his belly, and he stalks the gentle deer, snapping its spine with his mighty fangs. If the bear tells the cat that he wants to eat the deer, the cat tells him no. He takes the deer, but the cat spits and fights. Would you fight the bear?"

"No, Grandfather," Natty replied.

"The cat fights and is hurt and driven away. He wants his food and has fought for his food, but he does not hate the bear," the wrinkled old man said.

"Why doesn't he hate the bear?"

"The bear is bigger. He has more iron in his veins than the cat. His muscles are from the mountains, but he too, like the cat, has a wolf in his belly." The grandfather smiled and lit his pipe.

"But what if the bear took the cat's food, beat the cat,

and kept chasing the wounded cat for miles, taunting him and trying to kill him?'' Tracker asked.

"The bear will not do that. He searches for food, a squaw, and a place for his winter sleep. That is all," said the wise old sage.

"But some men will do that to other men," Natty replied.

The old man puffed thoughtfully on his pipe, then said, "The cat is smaller and weaker than the bear, so he must be smarter and faster. He must lay a trap and let the bear chase him to it. He must seek the help of the sky-people and mother earth. When he wounds the bear, he must chase the great beast and bite him many times. He must run him over the cliff and let mother earth kill the bear."

Tracker looked at his grandfather, smiled broadly, and said, "Thank you, Grandfather. You always speak so wisely. How can I thank you for your words?"

The old man stood slowly, walked past the fire, and stared out into the darkness of the surrounding trees. He walked back and sat down, accepting a cup of coffee from Tracker.

He finally spoke, while Natty sat, eyes transfixed on the oldster, "Ah, buy your grandmother a new satellite dish."

Natty laughed heartily while his grandfather relit his pipe.

A twinkle in his eye, the old man had said, "Make sure I can get the Playboy Channel."

Laughing to himself with the memory, Natty called Titan, sleeping on his bed, and they jumped on the elevator. He pushed the button.

Eight men parked their ATVs and built a fire not more than two hundred yards from the carcass of the buck the cougar had killed. One of them had a cooler on the back of his four-wheeler, and he had brought several packages of hot dogs which the would-be killers were now roasting over the campfire. One of the hitmen cracked a joke and some of the others laughed, then suddenly several fell face first into the fire or next to it. One grabbed his chest and looked down to see several inches of a crossbow bolt sticking out of his ribs. It was bloody, since it had already passed through the body of his friend across from him.

He was the first to stare into the eyes of Natty Tracker standing next to the big cedar tree. Something bloody but partially covered with leaves lay at Tracker's feet. What the man couldn't help but see, though, even at this great distance, was Tracker's light blue eyes staring at him. The eyes seemed to be getting darker. No, he thought, it wasn't the eyes, it was the woods—no, it was becoming nighttime. Why, he tried to reason, was the sun going down? As he slumped down into a sitting position, his dimming eyes stared at the fire. He smelled burning hair as his vision faded to blackness.

The other killers, all but one, ran to their ATVs, but only one managed to start his machine, before dying. The one man who was left ran through the trees screaming. He spotted a thick cedar tree and thought it might make a good hiding place. As he got up to it, he saw something buried under leaves and twigs. It was the partially eaten remains of the mule deer buck. He pictured a large mountain lion, lips drawn back, fangs bared. He yelped as Tracker stepped from behind the tree, and then he spotted Natty's light blue eyes. It was too late to stop or slow down, so the fleeing killer ran right into Tracker's Bowie knife, held waist high, and looked down at the handle being twisted by the powerful copper hand. He tried to scream, but it hurt so much he could only get a whimper out. He looked into the powder-blue eyes and then down at his own blood pouring onto the green grass below. He visualized the big cougar feeding on his dead body and then he died.

* * *

Rock Smith was scared. He had been bad all through school and in the Marine Corps. He was big and mean and was credited with more quarterback sacks than the rest of the team combined every football season in high school. This was different, though. This wasn't a bar fight on weekend leave or the hard hit on a running back. This was for real. He wondered what it would be like to die. He tried to imagine what it would be like to hold his breath and shut his eyes forever. Rock should have been thinking of security as he drove his ATV along the tree-line. He didn't, though, and he shot off the four-wheeler as Natty Tracker flew through the air out of a big bush and kicked him off the vehicle with a flying sidekick. The man's gun went flying and landed about five feet from his right hand. He reached for it, and there was a silver streak to his side. He looked at the steel jaws of a giant wolf closed down on his right forearm. He screamed in fear and pain, and a grinning Natty Tracker gave him a shushing gesture.

Tracker said, "Hold!"

Titan let go of the man's arm and immediately grabbed the man by the throat. Rock's eyes opened in abject fear and hysteria.

Natty said, "Pal, all I have to do is say the word K-I-L-L and you'll have terminal laryngitis. Now, I want the answers to several questions. First of all, what is your organization, and who's the boss?"

In a squeaky, raspy voice, Rock, said, "Reed Forest, the movie star, is the boss, and we're called SAFE-PEACE."

Natty said, "SAFE-PEACE? What the hell does SAFE-PEACE stand for? Titan rest."

The big dog let go of the man's throat and sat back on his haunches. Rock sat up rubbing his throat. He made several attempts to speak, but had trouble with his throat and voice.

Finally, he said, "SAFE-PEACE stands for Save the

Animals, Forests, and Environment—People Eliminating Atrocities Corrupting Earth. We are an organization that wants to stop the killing of the whales, of the fur seals, and of all animals. We want to stop the wearing of fur coats. We want all the idiots to stop destroying the ozone layer, ruining and destroying the rain forests, destroying the Earth with acid rain, industrial waste, and nuclear power. We want to stop the stupid world leaders who want to exploit and start wars just so their countries can profit by it.''

Natty looked at the big man sitting on the ground rubbing his bearded jaw and said, ''Very noble, so what the fuck's it got to do with fifty armed men trying to kill me?''

Rock, a little more animated after having been allowed to emote about his passion for saving the world, spoke a little more rapidly. Of course, it might have been the fact that he was staring at a pair of steel-trap jaws belonging to one of the creatures he wanted to protect.

He said, ''No offense, but there's a one-hundred-million-dollar bounty on you, and our organization needs money, big money, to carry on our fight.''

Tracker started laughing and said, ''Well, you dumb asses, the first thing you should invest in is an accurate information system, because the bounty on me was withdrawn. Secondly, you say you are out to save the world, huh? Well, how does that fit in with trying to take my life?''

Rock started to stand, but Titan's growl kept him in a sitting position.

He continued, ''The time for talk and minor demonstrations is over. We've decided that we had to declare radical action to save the world, and unfortunately, in any type of revolutionary action, some lives have to be sacrificed. Blacks didn't start getting civil rights in this country just because of Martin Luther King, you know.''

Tracker smiled and said, ''Funny, I don't see a Symbionese Liberation Army Day on anybody's calendar. You say that lives have to be sacrificed in a radical action. Why don't you just call it a war, instead of a radical action? Oh wait, I forgot, you want to kill people so we can have peace. You want to sacrifice a few lives so trees and animals won't get killed. I always heard men think with their dicks, but I swear, you and your friends must think with your assholes."

"Is it true that there's no bounty on you?"

Tracker said, "I don't have to lie to you. I can kill you anytime I want—and might just do that. Besides that, the bounty that was put on me and then lifted was put up by Muhammar Qadhafi and Saddam Hussein, both enemies of the United States. Why would you jerks even consider taking their money anyway?"

Rock said, "Because it's green money. It was nothing personal—we need the money. Our resources are running low."

Natty started laughing and smacked himself in the forehead, saying, "I don't fucking believe this. How many people are in SAFE-PEACE?"

"About two thousand, but we're growing," the man said.

"Two thousand people are running around with your mindset," Natty said. "Why doesn't the government know about your group?"

Rock said, "Because we have been meeting secretly and attracting new members by word of mouth, but we've only been in existence for about nine months, and we started with just forty-seven people. We're growing like wildfire."

Tracker sat down, smacked his crossbow against his forehead, and said, "I cannot fucking believe this, General."

The man looked all around and then figured that the wolf/dog must have two names: General and Titan.

Tracker continued, "What about Green Peace and Earth First and the other organizations who want to protect the environment in one way or another? What about the millions of Americans and others who really have very strong feelings about their causes but don't believe in killing people or trashing civilized laws to accomplish their goals? What do you suppose your organization is going to make a lot of them look like?''

Rock looked at Natty defiantly this time and said, "Sorry, we have to fight now to save our planet. There will have to be some sacrifices.''

Tracker was flabbergasted and angry, and it showed in his voice. "You dick! You stupid dick! *You* just became one of the sacrifices!''

The crossbow bolt went straight through the man's forehead, through the top of his spine, and disappeared into the ground behind him. His eyes crossed like they were trying to look up at the small hole above the bridge of his nose. Then he rocked once and fell backward onto a clump of loco weed. Titan, seeming to sense Tracker's emotions, walked over and sniffed the corpse, lifted his leg, and urinated all over the man's chest.

Tracker shut off the video sensor and stared off at the beautiful snow-capped peaks of the Sangre de Cristo Mountains. He felt pulses in his right leg, so he finally turned the sensor back on.

"Yeah, General," Tracker said angrily.

The deep voice boomed in his ear, "That was murder, Tracker!''

"Fine," Natty snapped back. "Then arrest me!''

Wally's voice smoothed a little. "Don't be ridiculous, Natty. You're one of few people in the world who really *can* get away with murder.''

Natty blew out some air and then answered, "The protection of the earth and its creatures is something very near and dear to me, General. It kept my red and black ancestors alive. I'm out here fighting fifty well-armed men who want to kill me. They declared war on me, and I cannot afford to take any prisoners. More importantly, they declared war on everybody who cares about the environment and our country. They're willing to collect a bounty on me from our country's two biggest enemies, so as far as I'm concerned they've declared war on their country also. I am against the killing of whales and baby fur seals and acid rain. I am against the destruction of rain forests and polluting the air and water. I do believe in controlled hunting, because I am a man of the wilds, and I've seen many deer that starved to death when hunting was banned in an area. I'm not against the wearing of fur or leather, because I believe that some animals are meant to serve mankind, but I *am* against some ways of obtaining furs. We are killing our own home because of greed and avarice and stupidity. The American Indians and the African tribesmen knew that the land and animals were there for us to exist, so they all practiced good common-sense conservation techniques, but modern civilization has done everything it can to destroy our environment. These assholes do not represent conservation. *I* do!''

Wally interrupted, ''Tracker, Tracker, okay—I get the point. I never heard you carry on like this. You're right. You're so extraordinary as a warrior, it's easy to take your fighting prowess for granted. You're fighting fifty heavily armed men by yourself. I suppose the Marquis of Queensbury Rules or the Geneva Accords are real noble but quite suicidal in your situation. You're the commander on the ground: I apologize.''

Wally Rampart, if he had never been anything else, had been a superb military commander. He knew that the man on the ground, in place, was always in charge, and nobody should try to judge or overrule his opinions, unless he was a complete incompetent or crazy.

Tracker said, ''General, they've declared war on me, on my principles, and my country. I take it back: You can call in the Army. Have them bring plenty of medevac helicopters and a whole load of body bags. See you.''

Tracker shut off the sensor. He took off at a trot in the direction of Lookout Mountain, jutting up out of the nearby tree-lined horizon. He kept feeling tingling sensations in his leg, but he ignored them. Natty went through one fence line, rounded a bend, and spotted two killers on ATVs driving away from him on the two-rut dirt road he was jogging down. He switched the lever on the crossbow to HS for heat-seeking, aimed at the left vehicle, and fired. He could see the bolt streaking through the air and the left ATV exploded in a giant ball of flame. The driver flew straight up in the air and came back down directly on the crown of his head. He was either dead or comatose when he hit the ground. Flames sprayed over the man on the right. Apparently he panicked, because the ATV took off at high speed. It suddenly exploded as he was trying to jump off, and he flew through the air. Then he lay motionless on the ground and burned as did the first one.

Tracker kept jogging and the mighty wolf/dog kept pace. He knew that the explosions would bring all of the other killers within earshot into the area. But with the invaders spread over two thousand mountain acres, some of them wouldn't be able to hear.

Tracker heard five ATVs before he saw them coming down the ridgeline to his left. He commanded Titan to sit, and he stuck the crossbow across his back on an angle. It held there on two Velcro patches.

The ATVs approached and Tracker stood, legs spread apart, with a lightweight Desert Eagle .44 Magnum semi-automatic in each hand. As soon as they were in range, Tracker opened up with both guns and the men flew backward off their vehicles. One of them took off, and, holding one pistol loosely in his left hand, Tracker held his left forearm up in front of his face and rested the right-hand gun across it. He squinted, zoomed his vision, and took aim at the one man who had managed to turn his ATV and start back up the hill through the trees. Right before the top of the ridge, Natty spotted a small patch of barren ground. Sure enough, the vehicle started to roar across it and Natty shot. The man, headless, flew off the vehicle, which went over the ridge, into the air, and landed in the top of a tree.

Tracker heard a low noise and whirled around. Ten ATVs, side-by-side, were roaring across the pasture directly at him. Some of the men were firing Uzis but were out of range. Natty quickly reloaded the two Desert Eagles, dropping the expended magazines at his feet. He slapped the forty-fours back into their holsters on his hips and snatched the crossbow off his back. He switched the lever to HE for high explosive and looked at the vehicles and then noted the distance on the tiny gauge in the corner of his eyesight.

He then looked at Titan and pointed at the nearby treeline and commanded, "Titan, *go.*"

The big wolf/dog looked at the trees and then at the men coming across the meadow toward Tracker. The beast sat still, ears pricked.

Angry, Natty said, "Titan, *go!*"

The giant wolf/dog growled deep in its chest.

Tracker snapped, "Fine, stay and get killed, you flea-ridden, dumb ass, sonofabitch."

Knowing he was being cussed, the big brute growled even more ferociously.

Tracker fired and missed with the first three arrows but connected with the next two. They exploded just in front of two ATVs, and the drivers went flying into the air in a somersault. One driver panicked and turned into the one next to him and they both crashed. Tracker switched the lever to S for standard and shot two more off their vehicles, but the killers were close now, and the silent weapon wasn't fast enough for Natty. He dropped the crossbow and whipped up both Desert Eagles and started emptying more four-wheeler seats. Tracker used up the whole magazine in each gun and didn't have time to re-

load. He dropped the empty guns as two more killers
bore down on him. Crossing his arms, Natty pulled out
a Glock 19 nine-millimeter semi-automatic from a shoulder holster underneath his left arm and another from underneath his right arm. He whipped the weapons up,
thumbed the safeties off, and then spotted a silver streak
from off to his right. Titan had crouched forward through
the grass but was smart enough to keep out of the line of
fire. He was now launching himself at the driver at Natty's right front.

Tracker realized this in an instant and aimed both guns
at the driver on the left and started squeezing off shots
rapid-fire. The man was so close he flew out of his seat,
and the vehicle shot past Natty. He turned to look at Titan
and saw the mighty wolf/dog's jaws covered with blood as
he stood over the prone body of the other driver. The area
where the throat had been was just blood and shredded
flesh.

Tracker whistled and the big animal ran over to him,
wagging his tail. The wolf/dog could see the big smile
on his master's face, and he could sense that he was going to get praise and not a scolding. He ran right into
Natty's arms and Tracker hugged him for several seconds
and petted him vigorously. Tracker was a warrior, however, and knew that emotions could be expressed later.
He dropped the magazines out of his Glocks and replaced
them with new seventeen-round clips. He then put an
eighteen round in each chamber, flipped on the safeties,
and holstered the two guns. Next, he cleaned off the Desert Eagles, reloaded them, and retrieved their spent magazines. He had not worked out a holster for additional
crossbow bolts, and he made a mental note that he was
running low on them.

Figuring that there were less than twenty killers left,
Natty beckoned his pet and took off looking for more enemy. The tall spy didn't have to wait long. He headed back
east on the two-rut dirt road and saw another pair of ATVs

coming directly at him. They were two hundred yards away across the meadow.

There were certain times when Tracker was dangerous, not as much to others as to himself. He would get so angry or rebellious that he just didn't care if he got wounded or not; he simply wanted to take the enemy head on. This was such a time, as the two attackers, apparently quite frightened by Natty's reputation, started firing at him from out of range with a MAC-10 machine pistol and an Uzi.

Tracker took off straight at the two killers yelling a wild war cry at the top of his lungs. They kept firing and charging at him, but their shooting probably wasn't quite as accurate as it should have been. Tracker just kept running and yelling, without even pulling a gun. They were so unnerved by this act of either the utmost courage or complete insanity that they didn't plan very well and both ran out of ammunition, because of panic firing, right before they reached him. His continued yelling and running totally rattled both of them so much that they skidded to a stop and swung the ATVs around and ran from the charging spy.

Tracker's hand went up into the back of his suit and swept out and down in an arc. His razor-sharp Bowie knife streaked through the air, flipped over several times, and stuck into the back of the neck of the driver on the right. The driver on the left turned his head and stared in horror, and the other one stood up, rose to his tiptoes with a scream of pain, fell over his handlebars, and was run over by his own vehicle.

The one on the left tried to turn and fire his weapon at Natty, but there was no round in the chamber. Something struck him from the left and he flew sideways through the air for a good ten feet and looked up into the snarling face of a gigantic wolf. He felt pain suddenly in his throat area and realized he couldn't breathe. He reached up and grabbed his throat with his right hand and looked at it totally drenched in blood. The killer tried to scream, but his larynx had already been torn out of his body. He saw the vise-like jaws start to engulf his face, and he felt tremendous pain in his eyes and cheekbones, but couldn't see anymore. At the same time, he heard bones crunching, and then he suddenly stopped feeling. He stopped hearing; he stopped seeing. He stopped being.

Natty fell on the ground, racking breaths struggling to pump life-giving oxygen into his spent lungs at the seven-thousand-nine-hundred-feet altitude. After he recovered his breath and stopped shaking, Natty went over and put one foot on the back of the one killer's helmet to yank the big knife out of the man's neck.

Tracker turned and started off across the meadow again and suddenly saw another thirteen vehicles roaring at him from the east. They were still three hundred yards off.

He said quietly, "Come on, fuckers, let's party."

Tracker pulled the crossbow out from behind his back and knelt down, resting his left elbow on his upraised left knee and carefully aimed. He shifted the lever to HE, squeezed off a shot, and one of the drivers exploded. Tracker repeated the action, and men started spilling off the wildly careening vehicles. Natty kept firing until he ran out of bolts, but there were still several vehicles charging at him, so he went to the Desert Eagles. Standing spread-eagled, he was now grinning and firing quickly, with killers flying off their vehicles and crashing into the ground left and right. Again, he dropped the empty guns and pulled out the Glocks. The Desert Eagles could easily penetrate the Kevlar vests of the killers, but with the Glock 19s, Natty had to aim at the faces, which was no easy matter.

Tracker killed all but two of the charging men. Titan took one as he had done twice before. Natty ran out of bullets in the left-hand Glock and dropped it in the dust and fired double-gripped with his right-hand gun. The last man was a monster whose gun had jammed. He must have stood six-feet-seven and weighed at least three hundred pounds. Tracker's right-hand gun clicked on empty, and the determined killer smiled as he bore down on the tall half-breed. Natty stood his ground, and at the last second, he jumped straight up and the man and vehicle passed harmlessly underneath him. The man had courage; Tracker had to give him that.

Natty stopped Titan from attacking as the behemoth skidded the ATV to a stop, jumped off the vehicle, and charged Tracker with a bellow. Natty stepped into a back stance. The big bruiser wasn't used to somebody facing him ready to fight and didn't know what to expect. He closed with Tracker, but the copper-skinned hero wasn't there. The killer felt a sharp stab in his ribs and looked down to see Tracker's foot snapping away from the three ribs it had just broken. The man hunched to one side, and he looked at the other foot just as it snapped into his nose and eyes. He heard his nose and cheekbone break and felt his legs start to give out from under him. Through a cloud of blood he saw a sadistic leer on Tracker's handsome face and saw a reverse punch traveling at his head. The speed was blinding, but to him it was coming in slow motion. He panicked but couldn't move quickly enough to slip the punch. The killer felt the fist crash into his temple, and he heard his skull break. Then there was a blinding flash, and suddenly he was in pitch blackness. He felt burning all over his body like he was in a blast furnace. The man was totally panicked now, and he felt his heart racing wildly in his chest. The burning was unbearable.

He screamed, "Where the fuck am I?"

He heard some laughing and then a deep voice said, "Hell."

Natty sat down and looked at his victim with the side of his skull crushed from the mighty reverse punch. The eyes were closed and the chest didn't rise and fall. The mountain breeze did stir the corpse's hair a little.

Forty-eight would-be hitmen had just died at Natty's hand, and the Tracker legend took another giant step. Their blood poured into the earth of the pristine mountain meadow and nourished the hungry soil.

3.

Love 'n' 'Splosives

DEE LIGHT LAY on her back in Tracker's large bed. Her red hair was draped over Natty's pillow and her own. Smiling, she looked out his bedroom window, past the Cheyenne Mountain Zoo, and stared at the tall statue of Will Rogers at the Will Rogers Memorial Shrine that jutted straight up at the end of the mountain ridgeline. Her eyes strayed back to Natty's massive muscular body, and they followed the lines of muscle, sinew, and scars down the ridgeline of his chest. She looked down at his navel and below, and a grin spread across her face. She thought about the shrine she had just looked at.

Natty turned and said, "Hungry?"

She looked down below his navel again and pictured the tall shrine once more. Her face got deep red.

Dee said, "Natty."

He laughed and said, "I mean, do you want me to go get us some food?"

The two lovers had been in bed all day and she was hungry.

"Sure."

Tracker, grinning, jumped out of bed, and she watched him as he walked out the door. Several minutes later, she heard Natty cheerfully whistling while he walked up the stairs. The naked spy walked in the door and Dee started laughing.

He had a scoop of vanilla ice cream, another of chocolate, some whipped cream, chopped almonds, and a cherry expertly arranged on his midsection. Dee giggled like a teenager.

He walked over in front of her with a cocky grin on his face.

Dee finally said, "Oh look, my favorite, a baby banana split."

Tracker pulled the can of whipped cream and some chocolate syrup from behind his back and loomed over her.

He said, "I can really get into dessert."

Dee enjoyed the sensation of the syrup being poured all over her and said, "I hope you do get into it."

Dee moaned and groaned while Tracker satisfied his sweet tooth. Her mind wandered back to when they first met.

He had been held by some killers dressed like ninjas in an abandoned warehouse in downtown Colorado Springs. Natty had been tortured and beaten, but had escaped by diving through a window head first, sailing in midair across an alley, and crashing through the window of another building, bullets following him all the way.

The building was pitch black, but that didn't bother Natty as his electronic eyes, even then, had a night vision capability. He ran to the exit stairway and padded barefoot down the stairwell. Going down three floors, Tracker emerged on the ground floor. The building smelled like the inside of an old coffin, and Tracker thought of this as he saw eight shadowy figures appear outside the building.

He whispered to himself, "He who hesitates gets his nuts shot off."

With that, the nude hero ran across the darkened warehouse and launched himself at a black shadow walking by one of the dirty opaque windows. Crashing through, Natty's shoulder struck the ninja on the neck, and Tracker's beefy arm wrapped around his head. The two smashed into a car parked along the downtown street, and Natty slid across the trunk with the ninja's neck snapping in the process, a flying tackle that would have made Dick Butkus proud. Natty quickly grabbed the Uzi off the man's limp shoulder and spun it just in time to spray two of the hitman's cohorts with a quick burst of automatic fire.

Still completely naked, he ran out in front of an oncoming car, pointed the Uzi at it, and held up his hand for the car to halt. The Pontiac Bonneville screeched to a halt, and Natty ran to the driver's door, jerked it open, and ducked just as two more ninjas appeared and fired bursts at him. He popped up and fired, knocking one down and sending the other for cover.

The driver huddled in a ball in front of the passenger seat as Natty jumped in and tore off down the road under a hail of gunfire. As he slid around the corner, he saw ninjas scrambling toward some parked vehicles. The passenger, wide-eyed and crying, sat up in the passenger seat. It was a ravishing redhead with a figure that would make Madonna contemplate suicide.

Natty said, "Excuse me, I normally don't dress this way when I'm out for a ride."

She stared at him with a shocked look on her face. Then it dawned on her that he was joking. Wiping her tears, she started laughing. Tracker grinned and started laughing himself. Her mirth verged toward hysteria, and she was soon roaring loudly with laughter. She pointed down at Natty's exposed penis, and he got an embarrassed look on his face as she held her sides laughing, tears pouring down her beautiful cheeks. He started laughing hysterically also. Bullets tore by the car, and they both looked behind them to see two vehicles giving chase, ninjas firing out the side windows.

The woman laughed even harder and squealed, "Now we're going to be shot to death!"

She kept laughing as Natty tried to speed up and avoid the pursuing killers. Despite this, Tracker kept laughing because of her hysterics.

Still howling with laughter, she said, "Well, at least if we get killed, you don't have to worry about getting bullet holes in your clothing like I do."

Natty grinned and slid the car sideways to the right around one busy corner and back to the left around the next. He looked over and she had begun to cry again.

Between sobs she said, "Are you a killer?"

Natty laughed and replied, "No, I was kidnapped by those people, and they were planning to kill me. They still are."

The young beauty thought for a minute and said, "I believe you."

Natty looked down at his bare body and grinned. "Why not? I'm telling you the naked truth. My name's Natty Tracker."

As he slid sideways around another corner, she held her breath and closed her eyes.

The car smoothed out and she replied, "My name's Deeann Light, but folks call me Dee."

Natty looked in the rearview and said, "Hang on."

He slid the car around another corner, tires smoking like they were on fire. Dee looked back as he quickly pulled over to the curb, and she saw two distant police cruisers speeding toward them, flashers and lights screaming in pursuit.

The two cruisers pulled up behind Natty, and the officers got out cautiously, hands on their pistol butts. All four of them walked toward the car slowly, as Natty held his hands up inside the car so they could see that he wasn't going to shoot. He also saw two sedans roaring down on the policemen from behind.

Natty rolled down his window and leaned out yelling, "Look out!"

The two cars of ninjas opened fire on the police officers and mowed them down. A short gun battle followed, but the cops, taken by surprise, were slaughtered. Natty shattered the windows of the ninjas' cars, and he took off, tires squealing. He looked in the rearview and saw the ninjas piling up to the two police cruisers. Tracker turned, sped down an alleyway, slid out into a one-way street, and headed in the wrong direction, running oncoming cars off the road. Then he slid right around the next corner. Natty saw that he was in downtown Colorado Springs, so he knew the streets pretty well.

"We'll go to my house near the Broadmoor," he said. "They've already seen your license number, so you're in danger going home."

"Can't we call the police?" she asked.

Tracker said, "You saw what happened to four innocent cops just now. They won't come to my house because they'll figure I'll already have help there."

"Who?" she asked.

"The Army, the Air Force, whatever," he said.

"Who are you?" she asked.

"Just a man," Tracker said.

Tracker looked over and caught her looking down at him. She got very embarrassed and covered her face.

Deciding to lighten things up, Natty queried, "Are you okay?"

She got a concerned look on her face and responded, "I'm scared, but I'm okay. What's wrong?"

Natty grinned, "Oh, you were just looking a little cock-eyed."

She turned and looked into Natty's eyes and the joke suddenly struck her. Her face got as red as her hair, and she buried it in her hands, laughing.

"I like your name," Natty had said. "Dee Light."

• • •

Tracker and Dee got up forty-five minutes later to wash away any food that may have remained on their bodies. Natty looked at Dee as she stepped out of the shower. She had the scars of a bullet wound in the chest, a bullet that had been meant for Tracker, but other than that, her body could best be described as perfect.

For a long time, Dee Light had led Natty to believe that she was a copyright/patent attorney practicing law in Colorado Springs and that their first meeting was a complete coincidence. When he had a "need to know," Dee had finally let Natty know that she was, in actuality, a U.S. Secret Service agent who had been personally ordered by the President of the United States to guard Natty Tracker. They had become lovers and good friends, which the President had told her was okay because Tracker would have become suspicious if Dee hadn't become his lover.

Natty had had other lovers, a few, but not too many, so Dee did not allow herself to be jealous. Her father had been a rancher and horse breeder in Colorado, and in fact, she had a beautiful Egyptian Arabian gelding named Shaheem that was a pasture-mate of Eagle. When she was younger, there had been one horse her father owned that couldn't be touched by anybody. They couldn't put a halter on him or rope him, much less break him for riding. Dee loved him because he was wild and free. She didn't try to halter the horse or restrain him at all. Consequently, he wanted to be touched, held, and ridden by her all the time. Nobody else could get near the horse. That horse was Shaheem, and she treated Tracker the same way.

Treating Natty that way had certainly paid off, because besides becoming lovers, she and Natty Tracker had become best friends. Tracker would not let himself fall in love with another woman while in the spy business, as he had lost too many friends as it was. In fact, just recently he had lost another lover, a PhD named Charity Case while they were scuba diving in the Bahamas. She had been shot and killed with a speargun by a man whom Natty had ended up feeding to a tiger shark.

Natty had previously fallen in love with a CIA operative also with a PhD named Fancy Bird. Fancy had been captured and brought to a prison in Tripoli, Libya. There, Natty had been shackled and forced to watch as the Cuban terrorist called The Ratel sodomized and raped Fancy. Natty had rescued her and the two were able to repay The Ratel and "give him his propers." They made it all the way to the harbor in Tripoli where Natty had discovered a good hiding place on a Libyan fishing boat. He had also recovered a rebreather lung from a previous infiltration into Libya and had been using it to move around underwater without detection.

Tracker looked through the bathroom door into his bedroom where Dee, still nude and smiling warmly, had just lain back on the bed and stared at him, a dreamy look on her face. He remembered that day in Tripoli harbor when he and Fancy had just made love and were looking forward to their return to freedom in the United States. Natty remembered that same dreamy look on Fancy's face as he had started to leave the boat to find food and turned to look back at her.

He had turned to her and said, "I'll be back in a few minutes. I have to go find us some food."

She lay on her back, still nude and sexy as ever, and just smiled at him. Her eyes opened wide and there was a loud bang. Tracker saw a large bullet hole appear between her eyes. Her body twitched once and she died. The man in the doorway had a sadistic sneer on his face as he pointed the .45 automatic at Natty's face.

"Amigo," the man had started to say, but was cut off by Natty's lunge punch and loud yell. The punch shattered the assassin's nose and was so powerful he flew backward off the boat and into the water. Tracker followed him out the door, a primal scream escaping his lips, but numerous shots from the dock and the shoreline forced him back. He caught a glimpse of the Latino swimming for shore as soon as he had surfaced. Libyan police officers had fired at him, and Natty knew that he must get away, but who was the Latin assassin?

Tracker knew that he had to save himself. He looked at Fancy's body lying lifeless on the bed, and he covered it with an old blanket. Natty realized that self-preservation had to take precedence over sentiment, and he knew that Fancy would have appreciated that. It was one of the rules of the game that they both had played by. In that fleeting moment, Natty also decided that he wouldn't be able to pursue the assassin, but he memorized every detail about him and would eventually hunt him down and kill him. He also made another promise to himself then: He would not even think about marriage or any kind of permanent relationship with another woman as long as he was in this business.

Grabbing his pack, he pulled out one of the MAC-11s, cocked it, zipped up the bag, and put the mouthpiece of the rebreather in his mouth. He made sure that he could easily reach his fins that he had strapped to the pack, and he moved to the door. Tracker flipped the selector lever on the machine pistol to full-automatic and took two steps out the door, firing as he ran and kept firing as he dived headlong into the water amidst a hail of return fire from the Libyans.

Underwater, Natty put the weapon in the pack, swam directly underneath the boat, and remained there. He knew they would soon have the shoreline swarming with frogmen, heat-sensing devices, vessels, searchlights, and maybe even trained dolphins like the U.S. Navy had secretly used in Vietnam to patrol for North Vietnamese saboteurs. He listened to the footsteps of cops coming onto the fishing boat for over an hour. He also heard the engine sounds of other boats cruising the area.

Two hours after the killing, Tracker slipped up the side

of the boat. Fancy's body was still there inside a body bag, and it was being guarded by a lone police officer. Tracker just walked down the ladder and straight up to the astonished cop. A word was never said; Natty simply side-kicked the cop at the base of the jaw and heard the neck break with a loud snap. The cop fell dead in a limp pile.

Tracker got Fancy's pistols and strapped on the holsters after removing the rebreather. He took the cop's gun and put it into his waistband, and opening his pack, he pulled out his camo jumpsuit and put it on. He decided to leave the MAC-11s in the pack until he had a chance to clean and dry them. He lightly touched the stiffening body in the black plastic zipper bag and went up the steps wearing the cop's hat. He walked off the end of the dock within sight of several cops and many soldiers, all engaged in various types of activity. To them, he was just a silhouette of a tall cop.

Tracker walked over to the nearest police cruiser, climbed in, started it, and drove away slowly. He looked in the rearview as he pulled away from the ocean and saw a flash a milli-second before he heard a bullet slam into the trunk of the small car. Tracker floored it and headed northwest along the ocean. His was the only cruiser close to the dock, so he knew that he had a little bit of a jump on them, but they finally appeared, a sea of flashing lights, in his rearview. Natty prayed for no helicopters, at least for now.

He turned south and roared through town. He saw signs indicating that he was on his way toward Tripoli International Airport, and he considered trying to go directly there and steal a plane or helicopter but then decided against it. He barreled down the boulevard and saw that the cars behind him were not really gaining by much.

The police kept after him and could see his tail lights far ahead.

The sergeant in the closest cruiser behind him called in and gave his location, speed, and direction. Preparations were made to set up several different roadblocks, including one to be set up with Soviet-made tanks. A pair of assault helicopters were warming up at Wheelus Airfield. The road ahead made a sharp turn to the right and the sergeant hoped that the American wouldn't make any turnoffs while he was out of sight.

The sergeant was soon rounding the same turn only to see Natty's car go airborne on the next bend. It exploded into a ball of flame in midair, did two somersaults, and came crashing down onto its top. Thirty seconds later, his cruiser and the others behind him skidded to a stop at the crash site. They couldn't even get close to the flaming tongues that licked up into the night sky.

If they had looked for it, they would have seen the rubber hose sticking out of the sand on the other side of the road and one hundred yards back from the site of the wreckage. It had been cut from the rebreathing apparatus which was now inside the burning car. The end of the hose in the soft white sand was still attached to the mouthpiece that was now inside Natty's mouth as he lay on his back, firmly pinching his nostrils shut.

Natty had made his mind up to survive. In fact, no contrary thought ever entered his mind. That was a given. He also hoped that his next assignment would place him in a country with more hiding places, so he could quit burying himself in hot, itchy sand. Tracker reached down and pulled a handkerchief out of a pocket, inched it up, and plugged his nostrils with it. Using the powers of concentration he had learned in his study of the martial arts and the patience he had learned from his grandfather, Tracker lay in the sand, unmoving, for three hours. He then dug his way out and crawled on his belly for another hour and took refuge in a small wooden shed that was being used to store dates.

After that, Tracker had stolen an old Army T-10 parachute and stowed away, not inside a plane, but on the tail section of a an aircraft heading out into the desert. He had jumped off and parachuted down to the desert floor when the plane passed close to where Natty's jet had been cached. He had made it to the plane and exfiltrated the country successfully, but only after making a bombing run on Tripoli harbor and dropping napalm on the fishing boat holding Fancy's body. She had been violated enough, and he didn't want anybody to see her or touch her, even though she was dead.

Afterward, he had killed Miguel Atencio, the hitman who had killed Fancy, when the man tried to assassinate the President of the United States at a football game between the rival Cleveland Browns and the Denver Broncos.

Tracker finished blowing his hair back into his tuxedo shag hairdo and started putting on deodorant and looked at Dee again as she lay across the bed. He pictured Fancy and Charity both in death, and tears welled up in his eyes. At that time, Dee just happened to open her eyes and look at Natty. A look of concern spread across her beautiful face, and she sprinted back over to the bathroom and grabbed Natty's massive arms.

"Natty," she said, "you started to cry. What's wrong?"

He was embarrassed and flustered and tried to figure out a way to cover up his vulnerability.

He finally said, "Oh, I was just thinking about how beautiful you are, Dee, and how much I treasure our relationship."

Her eyes searched his for a few seconds, and then a knowing grin spread across her face, and she said, "And you were thinking how you have already had two women close to you killed and can't bear to think of it happening again."

He dropped his head and shook it affirmatively.

Dee smiled and said, "Thank you, Natty, for the concern, but you don't need to worry about me. I'm not planning on dying just yet. Remember, when I'm not here with you on vacation or days off, I'm protecting the life of the President of the United States. I am *very* good at my work, and my job is to keep people alive. *I'm* included in that list."

He looked up and kissed her on the end of her nose, and she said, "Being a hero isn't as glamorous as they make it out to be in books and movies, huh?"

He shook his head negatively, pulling Dee into his arms and hugging her warmly.

She went on, "Tracker, I know I've got this scar from a bullet that was meant for you, but there were a lot more bullets that didn't hit me. If you'll look, you'll notice that you have some scars, too, and you're still here."

Natty didn't speak. He felt his manhood rising and pushing against her lithe body. She felt it, too, and they stared into each other's eyes. He reached down and swept her up in his arms and carried her back over to the bed and gently laid her down. After making love again, they went downstairs and swam for the rest of the afternoon.

Dee was a great companion and had been able to take a few days off from her job. When there had been a big bounty on Tracker, the President had made her the agent-in-charge of the Secret Service agents assigned to guard Tracker. Natty resented it, but he had personally saved the life of the Chief Executive, and the man was eternally grateful. Tracker had also proved himself totally invaluable to the government of the United States. Dee was indeed good at her job, probably the best.

The two finished swimming, and Tracker heard a beeping sound. He toweled off and walked into the recreation room, not far from the pool. Dee followed and saw Natty push a control button, and a video screen on the wall came on.

Tracker gave his voice-activated computer the command, "Rec room, outside security."

The screen immediately showed Natty's outside driveway and a black stretch limousine traversing it. He and Dee watched with interest as it pulled up in front of the mansion. They continued to watch as one of Tracker's security guards walked over to the limo and spoke both to the driver and the man in the back and looked at their identification. This preliminary screening was one of the additional security measures Tracker had taken because of constant attempts on his life. He felt that maybe security guards could at least screen out the flakes and the amateurs. He would then have to rely on his own instincts, inventions, Titan's intuition about people, and just plain Providence to provide the rest of his security.

While the driver waited with the limo, the man in the back, who looked to be a distinguished gray-haired executive walked toward the mansion, leather briefcase in hand. He rang the doorbell.

An electronic, computer-activated voice said, "Welcome. Your presence has been noted. Please be patient, someone will be with you momentarily. Thank you."

Tracker picked up a robe and tossed it on and then headed toward the front door. Dee followed, picking up her purse on the way. She opened the top and stuck her hand inside. Tracker stopped at a Duncan Phyfe antique table holding a Ming dynasty vase in the corner of the hallway. Natty knelt down and reached under the tiny throw rug under the table and opened a small trap door in the floor. He pulled out a Glock 19 nine-millimeter and stuck it into the waistband of his trunks at the small of his back. He then reached into the vase, pulled out his OPTIC System glasses, and opened the door.

The man smiled warmly and said, "Mr. Tracker, I am with NASA and I—"

While the man spoke, Tracker put his glasses on and suddenly snatched out the Glock 19 and rapid-fired three rounds into the man's chest. He kicked the still-standing body backward off the porch and dove back in the house, slamming the door with his other hand.

At the same time, Natty yelled, "Dee, Bomb! Down!"

Dee was indeed good, because, when Natty fired into

the man's chest, she had whipped her stainless steel Colt model 4519 .45 semiautomatic pistol from her purse along with two extra magazines. Clad in a bright yellow string bikini, she sprinted for the side door and just made it through when the plastic explosive in the briefcase went off. Most of the windows in the front of the house exploded inward, but the construction of the house, especially the front door, was designed to withstand such an attack. Out of instinct, experience, and training, Dee had held her left arm and hand up to protect the side of her head while she ran. She was untouched, although her ears were ringing.

Natty had done a racing dive and landed in a shoulder roll. During that brief time, he saw that Dee was almost all the way to the side door, so he knew that he only had to worry about himself. Coming out of the somersault, he dove straight into the dining room where Dee had been and landed in front of a big oak china cabinet just as the bomb went off outside.

Tracker heard the big limousine rev up and start to squeal out of his turn-around driveway. Then he heard rapid-fire gunshots and heard the car grind to a stop. He ran toward the front door, reached down into the trap door again, and pulled out a lightweight Desert Eagle .44 Magnum semi-automatic and some extra magazines. He went out the front door and dodged to his left and behind a pillar just as a bullet smacked into the door.

Tracker reached around the pillar without looking and sprayed the area where the limo was with searching fire from the Glock. He then peered around, holding the .44 with both hands, and saw what had happened. Dee had fired at the limo as the driver tried to pull out and immediately saw that it was armor-plated, so she quickly shot out all four tires. The driver had jumped out and shot Natty's security guard who had started to run up from behind. The driver was now using the car as a shield and was firing at Natty and Dee with what appeared to be a Browning High Power nine millimeter semi-automatic.

Tracker looked over at Dee, and she indicated that she was going to move to her right and go for a cottonwood tree about twenty feet away from her porchside position. Natty nodded and then held up his left hand. He used his fingers and silently counted one, two, three and jumped around the pillar and started rapid-firing the Desert Eagle at the driver. The man was a large muscular Latin, who ducked his head and waited for the firing to slacken a little.

In the meantime, Dee dashed across the lawn and dove behind the cottonwood. She rolled past it, fired under the limo, and hit both legs of the driver. He fell on his side screaming in pain, and Dee fired again and struck the forearm of his gunhand. The gun lay there, and he started to reach across for it with his other hand, but the sound of her voice stopped him dead.

"The next one goes between your fucking eyes, asshole!" she shouted, and he froze in place.

Dee yelled again, "Natty! He's covered and unarmed!"

Tracker started running and came around the car with his Desert Eagle stretched out at the end of both arms. Dee walked up, and the wounded driver looked up at her in the string bikini.

He said to Tracker, "She's the one who shot me, man?"

Tracker laughed and said, "Tell her that a woman's place is in a kitchen and find out, pal."

Dee looked over at Natty and grinned. He still had his OPTIC System glasses on and now removed them.

"Nice shooting."

"Thanks," she said. "How did you know the other one had a bomb?"

Tracker held up the glasses and said, "It had an electronic detonator and nine-volt battery. I saw it through the case."

She grinned.

Jaws agape, the driver on the ground looked at the two lovers and just stared from one to the other. The man started moaning.

Finally the man said, "You gonna read me my rights, man, and call me an ambulance?"

Tracker looked at Dee, laughed, and then said to the man, "Sure, you're an ambulance. You also have the right to die a slow, painful death if you don't tell me what I want to know."

Tracker cocked the pistol and pointed it at the man's head and said, "Do you understand these rights as I have explained them?"

Beads of sweat broke out on the driver's head, and he shook it affirmatively, eyes wide open.

Tracker said, "Where are you two from? Who sent you?"

The man said, "SAFE-PEACE. You know what it is?"

Natty said, "Yeah, I know."

He looked at Dee and said, "These idiots don't even know the bounty on me was cancelled."

The driver interrupted and said, "Yeah, they do, man. Reed Forest is scared shitless 'cause he fucked up and tried to kill you. He wants you dead just 'cause he's scared that you're going to get revenge on him."

"You know Reed personally?" Natty said.

"Yeah, man, I been his driver for two years."

Natty heard sirens approaching.

"You a member of SAFE-PEACE?"

The driver said, "Fuck no, man, I just work for Reed. That guy you blew away was supposed to be some kind of super hitman from La Costa Fucking Nostra, man. I don't believe in any of that stupid shit that Reed and his goofy fucking friends believe in. They believe in some weird fucking shit, man. Man, I'm gonna bleed to death."

Tracker said, "No, unfortunately, you're going to live.

No arterial bleeding, and the leg hits look like they went through your calf muscles.''

The man said quietly to Natty as Dee walked over to greet the police pulling in, ''Please don't tell them that she shot me, man. Say that you did it.''

Tracker laughed. ''Hell no, I can't do that.''

The man said, ''Why not?''

Natty said, ''Professional pride. I wouldn't have wounded you and left you. I would have put one right between those sweet innocent brown eyes of yours.''

Tracker smiled, aimed his forty-four between the driver's eyes, and pulled the trigger. The man screamed, and the police who were approaching shouted, but the empty gun only made a loud clicking sound. Natty laughed while the driver started crying, his chest heaving in and out. Tracker walked over to several Colorado Springs police officers who had pulled onto his property. He noticed that more officers were staring at Dee's body than were looking for evidence.

A big man came walking up Tracker's driveway, grinning broadly. Tracker waved at him and he waved back.

A Colorado Springs police rookie said to Tracker, ''Who's that?''

To which Natty replied, ''Soviet spy.''

The cop looked totally startled. Tracker grinned and thought back to an incident not long before.

He remembered when he had defeated the serial killer/arsonist called The Firefly. The President had assigned Secret Service agents to protect Natty because of the bounty placed upon him, and Dee was the head agent.

An assassin dressed like a ninja had been able to infiltrate Tracker's property and had unsuccessfully attempted to kill Natty. A report came back later that the ninja was actually one of the top hitmen for *Yakuza*, the Japanese mafia.

After taking care of the killer and figuring out how the

infiltration had been made, Natty and the agents had gone back into his mansion. Tracker invited everybody out to the kitchen, and he said he'd make them all tunafish sandwiches, potato chips, and iced tea. He heard some beeping sounds, gave a voice command, and the kitchen television screen came on. Natty looked at the screen and watched a large burly man walking down his driveway toward the porch. Tracker went over and dialed a phone number which had been written on the wall. He spoke quietly into the phone and then hung up.

One of the Secret Service agents asked, "Who is that, Tracker?"

Natty said, "A KGB agent who lives down the street."

All the agents except Dee jumped up and pulled out their weapons.

Natty and Dee both laughed, and she told them to put the guns away just as the front doorbell rang. One of the older agents, however, did keep his weapon out and hid in the pantry.

He said to Natty, "He may be a prince, but I have a job to do."

Dee looked at Natty and nodded her head affirmatively. Tracker walked to the door and let Yuri in.

When Natty had moved into the mansion, the government had sent a CIA man out to install scrambled telephones, and the KGB had sent agents across the country to follow the simple installer, knowing that he would only be going to the house of someone very important. Not long after, they started to spy on Tracker, usually using fake city street repair vans or trucks. They employed various devices for their electronic surveillance such as cone-shaped directional microphones that could pick up conversations just by the vibrations on a pane of glass. Tracker, however, had had double-paned windows installed with Muzak constantly playing between the inside and outside panes to make eavesdropping impossible.

Yuri was the head spy for the Soviets, so Tracker, as a joke, had Domino's pizzas delivered to the Russian spies while they were in their truck or van. It became kind of a joke between Natty and Yuri. After that the Soviets bought a house down the street from Tracker and put several spies in it to keep an eye on Tracker. The two men were heros in their own countries and had mutual respect for each other.

Tracker greeted Yuri warmly and led him into the kitchen. Yuri looked around the room without smiling, but gave Dee a big wink.

He said in a thick accent, "Hello, Miss Light, how are you?"

She looked a little surprised but then covered it up and replied, "How's the KGB?"

He laughed and said, "I wouldn't know."

Natty said, "Yeah right, Yuri, and I'm competing for Miss America this September."

Dee quipped. "Your boobs aren't big enough."

Yuri laughed loudly and pointed at her, saying, "Da, dat iss funny."

Tracker said, "You apparently know Miss Light. These gentlemen are my cousins. That one is Rufus. That's Waldo."

Yuri interrupted and said, "Da, Tracker, all your cousins work for U.S. Secret Service, huh? Iss good they put dees men, and Miss Light, to watch over you. Dat's why I come. We must speak private."

Natty took him into the other room, and Yuri said, "You must already know dat Saddam Hussein heard about money, death money, a bounty, da, bounty on you by Qadhafi. He got from, what you say, a, terrorists groups. All these help put one-hundred-million-dollar bounty on you in Swiss Bank. Everybody will come after you now. Cold war iss over, I like you. I tell you."

Natty clapped Yuri on the shoulder and said, "Thanks, neighbor."

A big grin spread across the Soviet's ruddy face.

Natty said, "Now, I've got a surprise for you. Have you had lunch yet?"

"No."

Tracker said, "Stick around a couple more minutes; I have something that will interest you."

Yuri said, "Okay, Tracker, I stay."

A few minutes later, after some small talk about the Soviet Union, Lithuania, and the consolidation of Germany, there was another ring on the doorbell.

Natty disappeared into the other room and then walked back into the kitchen, followed by a Domino's pizza delivery person. He set down a stack of red, white, and blue boxes full of hot pizzas. Natty paid him and tipped him, then opened the boxes and passed the pizzas around.

Then he got some soft drinks and light beer out of the refrigerator and passed them around. For about fifteen minutes then, a retired Soviet Red Army field grade officer, who was a war hero in Afghanistan, and was now a premier KGB intelligence agent, sat in the kitchen of America's top spy and ate pizza with him and a handful of Secret Service agents.

After ten minutes, Yuri stood up, just when the youngest Secret Service agent was thinking that he was probably a big, bumbling Commie who got drunk on vodka every night. The big Soviet picked up a piece of pizza and a glass of beer and walked over to the door of the pantry.

Yuri turned his head and smiled broadly. "I tink iss good for all of us to eat lunch, no?"

He opened the pantry door and there stood the older Secret Service agent, gun in hand, and Yuri handed him the food and beer.

While the group ate, however, different agents got up and left the room to check around the property and then returned to be replaced by another. They had all been briefed on Tracker's state-of-the-art security system, but the earlier infiltration had made them all doubly cautious.

Several detectives arrived from the Springs police force to investigate the shooting of the ninja, knowing that the Feds had already done everything.

Yuri got up to leave and shook Natty's hand with a very firm handshake. He shook with Dee and several of the agents. Tracker walked him out.

They stopped on the front porch and Yuri said, "You be much careful, Tracker. I like assignment. Good job to keep until retire."

Both men laughed.

Yuri got a grave look on his face and added, "You know of a terrorist called The Camel?"

Tracker said, "No."

Yuri added, "He iss wery deadly. Has long neck, sticks out, like diss. Has on his back, what you call like camel?"

Tracker said, "He's a hunchback?"

"Da! Dat iss it, a hunchback, like Quasimoto. Diss man iss wery wery good. He works for Saddam Hussein. If he comes at you, don't take any time to talk. Kill right then."

Natty patted Yuri on the broad shoulder and said, "Thank you, I will remember that. Come by again."

"Maybe," Yuri said. "Or maybe I get in trouble for coming today."

Then Yuri laughed and said, "Ha, well, if they get mad, what can they do? Banish me to America?"

Natty thought of the irony of the statement and laughed heartily.

After that, Natty had killed The Camel when he did make an attempt on Natty's life. He then put the body inside a pod and infiltrated Iraq with it, dropping the metal coffin through the roof of the palace Saddam Hussein was sleeping in. There was an intimidating note attached to

the body. The following day, the bounty on Tracker had
been withdrawn.

Natty watched the ambulance taking the limo driver
away, and he walked over and put his arm around Dee's
waist. She looked up into his blue eyes and smiled.

Tracker said, ''I have the feeling that those two aren't
the only ones who are going to try to lift my hair before
this is all over.''

4.

A Very Dense Forest

REED FOREST OPENED his eyes and moaned, which was now a daily habit. His heavy lids fluttered a little and through red-rimmed eyes he strained to look at the alarm clock. It nineteen minutes past noon. He reached for a bottle of Extra Strength Excedrin on his nightstand and popped two capsules into his mouth. The man looked around for something to wash them down with and found a half-empty glass on the nightstand. He swallowed the flat gin and tonic with the pills.

His eyes then looked down at the two naked women lying asleep on each side of him in the king-sized four poster. Both women were absolutely marvelous in beauty and physique. One was black and had long shiny black hair done in geri curls. The other was white and had short auburn hair in a kind of wedge cut. Both had shapely legs, flat tummies, and firm breasts. The white woman had shaved her pubic hair in the shape of a heart. The black woman was wearing a beautiful gold ankle bracelet and long dangly gold earrings, two in each ear. The white one wore a black garter belt with seamed smoke-colored stockings.

Reed shook his head and stared at them and then went

to the bathroom. He turned on the shower and stuck his head under the cold water, then yanked it out and toweled off, sputtering and cursing. He relieved his bladder, then walked over and brushed his teeth. Reed then took a swallow of mouthwash and turned his head back to gargle. He lost his balance and sat down on the commode seat, totally disoriented.

Reed regained his senses and stood up, looking into the mirror. He still had a handsome face, even after a night of boozing and drugging, following many more nights of the same thing. His tongue felt like it was covered with felt that had been soaked in stale beer and strawberry juice, even though he had just brushed his teeth and washed his mouth out. The six-feet-four-inch actor looked in the mirror, flexed his pectoral muscles, and frowned at the little roll of fat forming around his midsection. It upset him because he used to be so proud of his build when he was on his way up. He had enrolled at Gold's Gym and had really become obsessed with bodybuilding. Consequently, he really did have enormous muscles and was good-sized. Unfortunately, since he had become a major star, he just didn't seem to have the same hunger he used to have when he was struggling. He put his passions into two things: the organization called SAFE-PEACE that he had secretly founded with some of his ultra-liberal friends and partying like there was no tomorrow.

He looked into the bedroom at the two naked beauties and tried to remember where they had come from. Forest assumed he had made love to them, but he couldn't remember. His heart pounded with fear as he wondered if he had worn a condom. The actor didn't see any lying around, and then he wondered if he had even had intercourse with one or both of them. Then the star wondered why he couldn't remember what had happened. He worried that maybe one of them had AIDS. Reed laughed then and thought about his bodyguards. They screened all the women who were sent to Reed's bed.

"Besides," the star said to himself in the mirror, "who likes to wear a raincoat in the shower?"

He went into the bedroom cheerfully and awakened the two beauties. He took them both to the shower, and after they began to revive, they started to cheer up. A butler brought some coffee to the master bedroom and tried to keep his eyes off the ravishing bodies of the two women while he left the room.

Reed then had sex with both women, and all three went down to his pool for breakfast. Before they left, both asked him for an autographed picture. Reed Forest swam and lay in the sun to work on his tan until late afternoon. Steroid-pumped bodyguards and assistants of different sorts lounged and worked in the pool area.

After that, he picked up the phone and made a call to his nextdoor neighbor.

One of the bodyguards looked out the window toward the pool and grinned to himself as he listened to Reed's half-whispered conversation. "Those broads were just one-nighters, besides you and I aren't married or anything. We agreed that we can see other people, so come on over. I'll give you a massage, and besides I want to fuck you so bad I can't hardly stand it."

The bodyguard actually grinned and then hid it quickly as he heard Reed giggle like a child.

The star continued, "Okay, you know I'll do anything on a dare. Come on over. I'll see you in a minute."

Reed acted excited and ran upstairs to his bedroom. He changed into a brief bikini and ran over to the weight machine in the corner and started lifting weights. He looked at his biceps to see if they were pumping up. The excited actor then ran into the bathroom, splashed water over his face and body, and went back to the weights and continued lifting. He heard the doorbell and smiled. The crotch of his bikini trunks started pushing out as he heard his loving neighbor ascend the winding staircase. He heard his lover enter the room, sigh, and then drop a pair of black mesh bikini bottoms and a loose T-shirt.

Reed's heart was pounding from excitement and not exertion as he saw the naked shadow loom above his head. Thick lips came down over his and his heart skipped a beat as his lover's hands searched familiar territory. Reed was always tremendously aroused when his lover arrived. The man had played for the Los Angeles Rams for several years and was built like a Mack truck, but he was a sensitive lover. Incredibly, he and Reed were built so much alike and looked so similar, they could nearly pass for twins. Loving each other was more like the extreme in narcissism than homosexual behavior.

The two men made love the rest of the day, and the former football player finally went home after supper. The actor took a jacuzzi and then a shower and got ready for his bi-monthly meeting of SAFE-PEACE. His new limo driver picked him up in front of the house and whisked him down Beverly Drive to Santa Monica Boulevard. They turned right and headed toward the beach. On Ocean Drive in Santa Monica, they hung a left and followed the traffic down past the pier. Down the street they pulled into a motel on the left side of Ocean Drive, and the chauffeur got out to open the door for the young wealthy actor.

Reed Forest's parents had come from Schenectady, New York where his dad had been a jewelry store owner. Even then, before their move to Beverly Hills, little Reed got whatever his heart desired. His dad had spent most of his time at work and was a good enough man, but nobody in the family ever saw him. Reed's overbearing mother doted on him and gave him anything he wanted. He was not disciplined ever, and often caused problems at school just so he could watch his mother go in and raise hell defending him no matter what he was accused of. More than one principal and school board president received letters from the Forests' family attorney. It was just too much of a hassle so they bowed to the demands of ''the bitch,'' which she was called by many who had had dealings with her.

Mr. Forest had been one of the first investors in a company that made a new phenomenon: machines with computer chips and video monitors that displayed flying saucers and spaceships battling each other and little electronic monsters eating other things. They were called video games, and he had taken a real flyer on them. With the million he made, the family put Schenectady in their rearview mirror and headed west. The Forests were going to move into their new home in Beverly Hills, California, and rub elbows with the ''beautiful people.''

The first home was paid for with cold hard cash and cost two-point-two million dollars. Five years later, one of the beautiful-people friends-of-the-family who was into real estate listed their home for them and took in seven-point-six million for it from a Japanese businessman. She then moved the family into an even bigger estate, just a bit off Beverly Drive and not too far from the Beverly Hills Hotel.

Reed transferred to Beverly Hills High School and became friends with other kids who would soon grow up, like himself, to become today's stars. He was also a bit of a hyperactive youth and was always looking for something new to get into. Because of this hyperactivity, Reed attracted other students to himself, because they thought he was exciting.

Even in Schenectady, his parents had kept a bowl of one-, five-, ten-, and twenty-dollar bills on the kitchen table. Like cookies, they sat there for the lad to dip into anytime he needed a few bucks. This habit was continued after they moved to Beverly Hills, plus he received an allowance from Mommy and Daddy of three thousand bucks a month. His only task was to keep his room clean. Of course, the maid helped quite a bit with that.

The organization called SAFE-PEACE was borne out of Reed's lifelong habit of being an instigator and out of boredom. One day, he and two of his friends, both major young movie stars, were eating at Spago's, and one of them started talking about how pissed he was over the destruction of rain forests in Brazil. This started more discussions about peace on earth, the killing of seals, the destruction of killer whales, dolphins getting caught in tuna gill nets, and so on. The discussion then went on to an apparent inability of society to correct these wrongs.

The three movie stars had been friends all through high school, and Reed Forest had always been the leader. His parents had bought all three out of trouble when a sophomore girl's parents wanted to charge them with gang rape when they were seniors. The parents of the other two didn't even find out about the incident, so that endeared them all the more to young Forest. He had even paid for the girl's abortion out of either his pocket or the kitchen bowl money.

His two friends jumped at the idea when Reed said he knew how to make people aware. They would start an organization that would forget about protests and demonstrations and simply make some examples of people. Members were slowly added one or two at a time, and the group had grown, like Alcoholics Anonymous, privately and quietly by word of mouth. After the first killing, a fishing boat crew off the Pacific coast, they became wary about any members who might become too shocked at the terrorist tactics of the organization, so any ex-member would become an ex-member of the living.

Reed Forest walked into the banquet room at the hotel along Ocean Drive. There were many other members and everybody acted excited to see him. Others just were excited because he was a celebrity, so they would sidle up to him and a minute later walk away, brown goo oozing off their noses. The wife of one of his friends walked over and gave him a kiss, a little too long to be friendly, and whispered something in his ear that made him giggle. The friend noticed this little exchange and became quite jealous, not of his wife, but of his friend and lover, Reed Forest. Apparently, the young actor found cookie jars to dip into everywhere.

Reed moved over to the table set up on one side of the meeting room and helped himself to a small plate of hors d'oeuvres. He then picked up a martini at the corner bar.

Ten minutes later, Reed moved to his place in the chairman's spot at the head table, and everyone had a sit-down dinner followed by a short polite meeting run completely by Robert's Rules of Order. The minutes were read, and the treasurer's report and committee reports were given. Afterward, the meeting adjourned, and Reed stood up and announced to everyone that he was hosting an impromptu party at his house and all were invited.

In less than an hour all of the guests had arrived, and miraculously, everyone from the meeting came to the party, including one of the newer members of the club, Dominic Lombardi. Dom had joined the organization just a month earlier when invited by an acquaintance who always billed himself as the "executive marketing rep for coke supplier to the stars." He had attended several meetings and acted enthusiastic about the group's goals.

Dom hated California. He hated sunshine and surf-boards, blond babes, and beach volleyball. Dominic loved Coney Island hot dogs with everything, subways, the sense of survival that comes from negotiating the New York experience, the smell of bus fumes, and the far-off sounds of sirens and car horns. In L.A., his adrenaline seemed to be at rest, but in the Big Apple, Dominic felt alive and in touch with himself. He had promised himself a transfer back to the big city as soon as possible, but the FBI was sometimes a cruel taskmaster, and he had been assigned to the branch office in Beverly Hills.

Like many FBI agents, Dom had started out with a degree in accounting and a minor in police science. He served a short term with the police in his native Brooklyn and then became a Fed. He proved himself in several undercover sting operations and went deep undercover in Brooklyn on a joint operation with the DEA. Because of several suspicious occurrences, the agency had decided to place a man in Reed Forest's organization.

Agent Lombardi had gotten into the group through a coke dealer, whom he considered a complete snowed-out asshole, but he had been treating him like his best friend. So far he had only been invited to attend the meetings themselves at the Santa Monica motel and had not been invited to the after-meeting get-togethers. This night, however, he was going to go to the home of the "Chief Asshole," Reed Forest.

There was a major problem in this, however, and that problem was in the form of a five-feet-three-inch, one hundred and forty-two pound brunette named Norma Rae Ledbetter. Norma Rae, thirty-four years of age, was the mother of a normal fourteen-year-old boy and a cute twelve-year-old girl. Born in Fort Wayne, Indiana, she had married a man from the First Methodist Church, where her family had gone for years.

Her husband graduated from Ball State College where she attended for one year, and then he became a sewing machine salesman in her hometown. He was a good worker and got promoted to store manager before very long. Norma Rae was what you would call an average American woman.

That is, until her husband got transferred to a much bigger store in the Los Angeles area. It was great for the family, but the cost of living in LA was much higher than in Fort Wayne, Indiana. Even with her husband's raise, Norma Rae needed to bring in money also. She had taken a government test and passed a BI (Background Investigation) and was soon working for the FBI in the Los Angeles area as a secretary.

The way that this affected Dominic Lombardi was simple. The cocaine habit that Norma Rae had acquired almost instantly in college, when her roommate and best friend coaxed her to try it, finally caught up with her when she failed to pass a spot urine test. She was summarily fired, but not before learning that Dominic Lombardi had been brought in as a special agent who was going undercover to infiltrate SAFE-PEACE, an organization she had heard about that had celebrity involvement. As far as she knew, SAFE-PEACE had supposedly been responsible for the serious injury of a logger in Washington who tried to cut down a tree with a spike in it. His chain saw had broken on the spike and swung around to cut off the bottom inch of his chin. It was unfortunate, but she thought it was a McCarthy-type tactic to infiltrate an agent into an environmental protectionist group.

That was her rationale when Norma Rae passed on the intelligence about Dom to her coke supplier, who was also a member of SAFE-PEACE. When the man learned that she was a secretary in the FBI, he had promised her that he would give her free blow if she gave him any information the FBI acquired about SAFE-PEACE. She listened to a long lecture about how his organization was indeed a little radical at times, but he told her they were simply involved in trying to save the planet and its creatures. She turned down the offer quite emphatically, but then she hadn't yet gotten back into nose candy in a big way.

She had not done any coke for a year and had been proud of herself, but a convenient excuse finally came up and she was on her way again. The dealer had promised her that his group was harmless, so if they found out about investigators or anything, they would just know to stay away from those people. To her, the little she told the man was well worth the nice plastic bag full of entertainment she received, and nobody would get hurt by it. In fact, she figured, if she wanted to do some blow occasionally to feel better, who could it possibly hurt? Norma Rae's husband and kids had no idea that mommy was a "stoner."

Reed Forest had different plans for Special Agent Dominic Lombardi. He was going to do a bit more about him than just ignore him. In fact, the organization called SAFE-PEACE was going to send a strong message to all the "war-mongering, polluting, earth-destroying ultra-conservatives who permeated society."

Reed's mansion, guesthouse, poolhouse, stable, and grounds reminded Dom of movies he had seen featuring famous Beverly Hills stars' mansions. In fact, he thought he had remembered having seen it on a segment of "Life-styles of the Rich and Famous."

When the caravan of cars and limousines arrived at the mansion, they spilled their human cargos out, and people were soon gathered everywhere in small groups. This gave Dominic a good chance to move about the property and do some good reconnoitering. Champagne flowed freely and trays of hors d'oeuvres were being carried here and there by white-gloved butlers who looked a bit burly for the run-of-the-mill gentleman's gentleman. Special Agent Lombardi worked his way into the house and toward the area where he figured the office might be.

He moved through the library where a young man who looked like a reincarnation of John Lennon was passion-ately kissing a young lady dressed in the manner of Diane Keaton. He had lifted her long, Goodwill Store skirt up and slid his hand up underneath to search for hidden an-tiques or even fresher surprises located between her thighs. At the same time, the two kissed each other with a passion that indicated promises of "strawberry fields forever."

Dom passed the two lovers and moved through a large brass-handled door into what he had been searching for, a walnut-paneled office with walls lined with shelves con-taining books and ledgers, as well as trite awards and trib-utes the star had received from around the country. He moved to the impressive desk that looked like something a nationally renowned attorney or corporate CEO would sit behind, and he tried to open the top drawer.

The rustle of clothing behind him warned him.

Dominic Lombardi had not started out as a "wimpy accountant" as some local-yokel cops referred to FBI agents. He had grown up in New York's Little Italy, and had many childhood buddies who had taken a more traditional path in life than he had. They worked in various positions for *La Cosa Nostra*, and a few had been killed or were serving prison sentences. One of the reasons Dom had become an agent was because of the pride he felt about being Italian. He was indeed sick of seeing every successful person who had a vowel at the end of his family name gossiped about as being a *mafiosi*. He had considered running numbers to save up money for college when he was a teen, but instead opted to spend his time working on earning a football scholarship. The young Dom had pumped a lot of iron as a teenager and had "run the bleachers" more than a few times in an effort to reach his goal. He had become an all-state linebacker and also held the city record for punt and kick-off returns, having run back two hundred-yarders on kick-offs and a ninety-two-yard punt return during his senior year. He was also an all-conference wrestler his junior and senior years. The agent had kept in good shape. If he put his hands on something, it generally moved.

That was the main reason the two pairs of hands that had grabbed him could not hold him. He lunged forward and faced his attackers, two burly men in butler's uniforms who had been apparently hiding in a small half-bath slightly to the left and behind the massive desk. Both were grinning and Dom knew he had been had. One came at him, tree-limb arms spread wide. Dominic stabbed him with three short jabs to the chin, bent him over with a kick to the base of the right kneecap, and then straightened him up with a right uppercut that was launched from the hip. The man went straight up as if launched from Cape Canaveral, peaked out on his tiptoes, and toppled over backward. Not waiting for the other man try something, Dom

waded into him and rained blows on his face, tattooing
the brute with bumps and bruises while receiving only one
slight stinging blow himself. A right hook to the temple
sent that man, also unconscious, to the floor.

Dominic Lombardi knew he had been had. He had been
set up and would have to get the hell out of there, fast. He
bent over and reached up under his trouser leg to grab the
comfortable grip of the snub-nosed Smith and Wesson
Model Ten .38 special revolver he had in his ankle holster.
Just as his fingers wrapped around the gun, however, he
saw giant fingers as they closed down over his shoulders
and then snatched him up into the air and sent him flying
across the giant desk, as if he were a stick tossed in the
air by a frisky Golden Retriever. As he sailed across the
desk, he looked back into the sadistically grinning face of
Goliath himself.

The giant's name was July Jefferson, and Dominic knew
in that split-second who the man was. Fourteen years earlier July had killed a West German millworker in a bar
fight in Manheim, Germany. The killing had been accomplished with the big man's bare hands, but of course, he
was only eighteen years old at the time and hadn't reached
his full height and size. At that time, the young U.S. Army
spec four was only six feet six inches tall and two hundred
and eighty-seven pounds of muscle, anger, and meanness.
He had since filled out and had grown two inches taller.
July had been charged with manslaughter in the killing and
had spent several years in the Fort Dix, New Jersey max-
imum security stockade until he was finally released and
booted out of the military.

After being dishonorably discharged, July got a job on
the docks in New York as a longshoreman. The giant black
man didn't get along with anybody, and he loved to fight.
Consequently, he spent many a night in jail for bar fights,
street fights, and so on, until he moved uptown from his
native Harlem. A Manhattan restaurant owner who acquired millions by smuggling cocaine hired July as his

head bodyguard. The big man had also become head en-
forcer and executioner and had been questioned by New
York's finest in more than one killing. His victims usually
were found with many broken bones and, more often than
not, several fatal injuries. July was never one to stay too
long in one place, and his love of inflicting pain and torture always made his employers less than distraught about
his decisions to leave, so he had moved to the land of
glamour after Reed Forest saw him and hired him on the
spot as his head of security.

Dom's service revolver had gone flying when he was
tossed across the desk and was now lying against the far
wall. The monstrous bodyguard walked toward him slowly,
and the G-man tried to figure out what to do. His left leg
felt broken from his crash landing but he had a neck to
protect.

Once in a game against a crosstown rival, there was a
sweep to Dominic's side and a big lead blocker had speared
the young Italian lad with his helmet, fracturing the bone
in Dom's lower leg. Filled with adrenaline, Lombardi had
shoved the man face first into the ground and launched
himself over his body and through the air like a human
missile. His shoulder struck the tailback squarely in the
breadbasket and stopped his run in midstride. His feet hit
the ground and he drove the runner up in the air and backward while he pulled on the back of the running back's
thighs with both hands. Dominic had hopped off the field
on one foot and fell on the sidelines in pain before the
running back even was able to breathe again, let alone
stop seeing stars.

A broken leg was not going to keep the now-older Lombardi from taking on the killer beast approaching him. He
got to his feet and swung a series of hard lefts and rights
into the big man's stomach and ribcage. With a bass voice
that had to have come from Hell, July just laughed, then
dropped his arms, and stuck his face forward. Dominic
punched him right on the point of the chin with a hay-

maker from left field. The results of the powerful punch were strange; Dominic Lombardi felt what seemed like an electrical shock that numbed his arm all the way from the hand up to his shoulder, and it even started to give him a headache on the right side, but all it did to July was produce a deep belly laugh. He then swung his own haymaker, and Dom, seeing it coming, threw up both forearms to block it, and the punch drove the forearms back into Dom's handsome face while he flew backward and slammed into the far wall with a crash. He was dazed as he felt those giant hands grab him again and carry him somewhere, half-awake and half in lala-land.

By the time Dominic regained his faculties, he realized he was standing naked in front of Reed Forest and the entire group of men and women, some of whom were now giggling at his nudity and also out of nervousness. July had a hold of his arm and there were several other bodyguards around holding automatic weapons.

Everything then became a daze as the frightened but courageous FBI agent heard Reed lecturing the group on making examples, especially of snoop government agents. Reed also focused on how Dom's remains would help to replenish the earth and the soil from whence we all came. Dominic was then covered with a metal chest and back protector from a medieval suit of armor. Next, cotton was stuffed in both of his nostrils and he was forced to stick a snorkel in his mouth. It was attached to a length of garden hose. His fate was finally starting to hit him, and Dom struggled with all his might while many hands clutched him and turned him upside down.

He spit out the mouthpiece and nervously quivered, "What's the armor for?"

Reed, upside down in his view, said, "Why, to keep your chest from being crushed, Agent Lombardi. We want you to enjoy the earth as long as possible."

Dom's eyes opened wide as the mouthpiece was replaced, and then he saw the hole in Reed's garden. He was being moved toward it and was now over it. The gaping black hole was right in the middle of some rose bushes and looked to be at least six feet deep and was only wide enough for his shoulders and the armor breastplate. Dom started to scream but checked himself as he was dropped head first into the grave with the air hose held out above ground. The last thing Dom heard was Reed's laughter and some women gasping. He immediately felt cold wet dirt shoveled on top of his upside-down, naked body, and he tried to control his breathing, his survival instincts taking over after the hard years on the streets of Hell's Kitchen. Even with the cotton in his nose, he could smell the fresh dirt and was doing okay until he was no longer able to move his arms or legs or anything but his lungs. Dominic Lombardi was upside down, buried alive, and the full impact was now hitting him.

He remembered Reed Forest saying that at least he could, in death, now tell the whole world to kiss his ass, and he remembered nervous laughter. Dom tried to scream but couldn't. He tried to cry but his eyes were forced shut by the crushing dirt. His heart started pounding so fast that he thought it would explode. The blood was rushing through his head on top of that, and he knew he was going to go insane before he died.

Then a calmness and a resignation suddenly overcame him. Through his feet, he could feel vibrations coming from people walking on the ground above him, but Dom didn't care. He was going to die soon, buried in the dirt of the state he hated so much. He fainted, but the blood rushing to his head revived him immediately. The panic returned and he wanted to scream. The FBI agent tried but he couldn't. He tried to wiggle his toes and fingers but nothing would move. He voided his bladder and felt the warmth from the urine in the dirt.

Dominic thought about the new device that the FBI had issued him. It was called the KEEPTRACK System and had been developed by some superspy. It was some kind of microchip beeper device inside the handle of his Smith and Wesson Model Ten. If an agent were going undercover into a dangerous situation, all he had to do was call in to headquarters and they turned on a radio receiver that received a beep on a select frequency once every minute. He was also required to squeeze two small round gold plastic shields in the handgrip twice. Under the gold circles were two microchip sensors. If the agent didn't squeeze the sensors at least once every fifteen minutes while on the mission, the receiver would start an alarm sounding at headquarters. Before heading for the meeting, Dominic had, as usual, called in to headquarters. It had been two hours now since the last time that he had pressed the gold shields on his gun, which was now lying in the fake bottom of Reed's desk drawer.

He had no idea of how long it had been since he had been captured. In fact, Dominic was barely sane, but something in him, something from the streets maybe, made him hold on to a slim thread of hope. He talked to himself and tried to remain calm. Every few minutes he started to panic again, but he knew he had to make it.

Dom suddenly remembered his father and his alcoholism. His dad had caused a lot of problems and heartaches for a number of years because of a drinking problem, but Dominic's mom kept her mouth shut. She was a loving, dutiful wife, but she also showed no sympathy either. Once, his dad got busted for DUI and got tossed in the drunk tank. When he made his allowed phone call, it was, of course, to his wife of many years. She told him to call his bar buddies to bail him out, but she wasn't wasting their grocery money on such folly. About two months after that, his dad suddenly announced that he was an alcoholic and was going to do something about it. He became an active member of AA.

Dom really admired the old man when he watched how the man silently suffered through the first year, but he never drank again. When Dom was going through a rough time in the police academy while torn between two girl-friends, he and his dad had taken a long walk one week-end. It was the most emotionally upsetting time in Dom's life, and he didn't know what to do. His dad spoke about that first year of sobriety and told Dom that many times he would try to make it through one day at a time. He said that sometimes, it was so rough, that he had to just pray and try to get through each hour without worrying about the next hour.

Dom thought about that discussion, and he decided that he would just get through ten more minutes. If he could make it ten minutes more, then he would worry about the next ten minutes.

Reed was talking to a young starlet by the swimming pool while others kept drinking, snorting, and partying hard. Two couples were now naked and cavorting in the swimming pool playing underwater tag. They heard a noise and looked up above them and all other eyes turned sky-ward.

A drunken LA attorney said, "It's a fucking UFO!"

A strange craft was descending slowly straight down above the swimming pool. One of the bodyguards pulled a MAC-10 machine pistol out from under his coat, but a signal from Reed made him holster the weapon. The tiny craft was black against the night sky and was making a popping sound along with the noise of a small engine like a lawnmower's.

As it got lower, everybody could see that there was a pilot in a black flight suit and he was wearing a helmet. As he turned his head either left or right, an M-60 ma-chine gun mounted on an electronic head turned with the pilot's movements. The craft was a helicopter but it looked like it was built on an overturned whitewater raft. It hov-ered above the pool which the naked couples were quickly vacating and then rested on the water's surface. While ev-eryone in the party stared in wonder, the pilot then pulled back on a large lever next to his single bucket seat. The rotors started spinning freely, now disengaged, and another engine noise now came from underneath the craft. In seconds, it rose up about a half a foot above the swimming pool's surface. The pilot drove the strange vehicle over to the edge of the pool. He shut it down and it floated next to the diving board and then, removing his helmet, the tall man stepped off and tied the Hovercopter to the diving board as if he had just come in from a morning of bass fishing and was mooring his boat to a dock on his own private lake. Natty smiled as he thought back to his first dangerous foray with the Hovercopter.

Natty had parked and hidden his F-15E Eagle jet one hundred and thirty miles out in the Libyan desert and was going to use the Hovercopter to infiltrate in close to Tripoli and to the infamous prison where his former flying mate, Rabbit Peters, had been kept prisoner until Natty had saved him. Tracker was going back to kill The Ratel, the notorious international terrorist who had tortured him and had cut off his left ring finger in the process.

The flight had been uneventful until he was a short distance outside Yefren in the area called the Gebel Nefusah. As he cruised aloft, his revised Tracker device on his left wrist started flashing. Natty set down and in a few minutes had transferred to the hover mode. The device indicated that multiple targets were two clicks to his front. He went forward at full speed and had them in sight within a minute. They saw him, so he stopped and set down on fine tan-colored sand, clouds of it blowing up all around the Hovercopter.

Natty looked at the group of men and squeezed the frame on his glasses. He zoomed in to look at a Soviet T-72 battle tank, two Soviet BMP-76 armored personnel carriers, and the column was led by a British Ferret armored car. Tracker figured that they were out on maneuvers or convoying somewhere to go on maneuvers. In either event, he knew that they had to have weapons with live ammo with them or they wouldn't be out in such a deserted area. Natty realized that they did have radios, and those had to be silenced. The $64,000 question was: How? Natty had a grenade launcher, a light machine-gun, and two machine pistols. Facing a Soviet BMP-76 tank, Natty might as well have had a slingshot and a pellet rifle.

The column was several hundred yards away and headed straight at him. He saw somebody looking out of the armored car with a pair of binoculars, so he smiled broadly and waved. The man in the car also smiled and waved back. Tracker quickly reached into his pack and pulled out a bottle of alcohol kept in case of wounds. He poured it out and quickly poured gasoline into it from the gas can and then shoved a sock into the bottle's neck. He climbed back into the Hovercopter, put it in flight mode, and took off after first lighting his Molotov cocktail. He immediately flew at the soldiers who were obviously puzzled. He hoped that they had not radioed into headquarters yet. Still waving and smiling, he pulled into a hover twenty feet above the tank. By now, men were waving at Natty from each of the vehicles.

He smiled and produced his expedient bomb and dropped it directly on the air louvers above the tank's engine. The flaming liquid made its way down into the engine compartment. Natty bit the M-60 trigger mechanism and hosed down the wavers below before they realized what was happening, and then he concentrated on one goal: knocking out the radio antenna on each vehicle. He accomplished this by firing rifle grenades at almost point-blank range. Bullets tore at the small craft from both APCs. He turned sharply, pulling out his left-hand MAC-11, and with that and the M-60, he wiped out both machine-gunners. He felt several bullets brush past his cheek, but miraculously, his craft was essentially untouched. He then started firing the M-79 grenade launcher and finally disabled each vehicle. A bullet came up through the platform, and

Natty screamed in pain as it tore through his right thigh. He got angry. No, he got pissed. Men started piling out of the crippled vehicles and fired up at him, taking refuge behind the steel monsters. Tracker dived straight at the gunfire, biting down with his teeth, and firing the MAC-11s left and right, and then with his right hand he hit the tiller trigger four times as quickly as he could and launched four grenades. He swept in so close that as he passed over, a piece of shrapnel from the last grenade flew up and put a razor-sharp cut in Natty's forehead and imbedded itself in the front of his helmet lining.

Tracker's thigh burned and ached. He put it out of his mind, but he couldn't ignore the blood that was now flowing into his eyes. He headed straight away from the action and flew to a distant sand dune where he set the chopper down. Natty unhooked his safety harness and jumped out with the out-of-range Libyan soldiers taking a sporadic "Hail Mary" shot at him.

He reached back and grabbed the plastic gas can and placed it next to his seat. He reached into the pack and pulled out a T-shirt, tore it into strips, and wrapped one strip around his thigh and the other around his forehead. He then took off directly at the remaining soldiers. They began firing before they should have, but Natty wasn't even noticing. He grabbed the can of gas and unscrewed the cap. Braving the shooting, he plunged straight ahead firing the M-60 with his teeth. Closing in on the remaining Libyans, Natty made them all duck for cover by firing the M-79s again. He pulled back when he zoomed in over their heads, and lowered the tiny aircraft to a hover, counting on the downblast from the rotors to keep the soldiers' heads down. Luckily, he was correct. Hovering, Natty held the steering tiller between his knees and poured the gas over the screaming soldiers and vehicles below.

He pulled out of the hover and circled quickly, bullets flying at him, while several, sensing what was coming, tried to run. Natty buzzed over them and fired a flare gun to ignite the gas in a giant ball of flame. He had to hold the tiller tightly because of the concussion. This was followed by two secondary explosions when the ammo in one APC and the gas tank of the armored car both exploded. Natty set down and carefully got out of the helicopter.

Holding both MAC-11s, Tracker walked cautiously forward and found that all the Libyan soldiers were dead. Natty just stared into the flames and looked at the dead bodies. Anybody who claims to be a warrior and has looked at his enemies fallen before him without feeling remorse is either a liar or sick. Tracker felt saddened, very much so, but he had a mission to accomplish, so he shoved his feelings to the recesses of his mind. It was filed there in his memory, to be brought back up at a future time when it would be safer for him to deal with it.

That thought hit him now for it was certainly not a safe time to reflect on the past. He had calmly and coolly entered his enemy's camp. While party-goers and bodyguards alike stared in amazement, Natty Tracker walked over to the handsome star Reed Forest. Tracker's right hand shot out and caught the superbrat by the lapels. He jerked him one-handed forward and up onto his tiptoes. At the same time, Natty heard guns being cocked, and his left hand suddenly had a Glock 19 nine-millimeter automatic in it. It was cocked, and he shoved the barrel into Reed's mouth and then grinned evilly.

"You've been shooting off your mouth a lot," Natty hissed quietly. "Unless you want some help with that, their guns better get put away quickly."

Reed Forest had heard too many things, incredible things, about Nathaniel Hawthorne Tracker, and the hard stare from the powder-blue eyes that now bore into him made him look away uneasily.

He quickly shouted to his bodyguards, "Put the guns away."

Tracker grinned and said, "Pleased to meet you, Mr. Forest. Name's Natty Tracker."

Forest said, "I know."

Tracker said, "Now, let me tell you why I'm here. We're going to have a production. You're the star and I'm the director. Now, I'm torn between two titles, and I'm going to let you decide which one to name the movie. One title is *Temporary Salvation* and the other is *Death of an Asshole*."

Reed Forest gulped deeply and his heart pounded wildly.

Natty continued, "Now here's the scenario. An undercover FBI agent disappears—here, tonight—and the hero— that's me—shows up to find him."

Did he detect a hint of a shocked look on the handsome face of the actor?

Reed Forest had hidden it, he knew, but how the hell did this Tracker know about Lombardi, and how did he get here so quickly? There must be somebody else here who called him or the FBI on the phone or radio. Then he thought that that made no sense because he apparently didn't know where Lombardi was buried or even that he was buried.

Tracker went on, "So the hero asks the villain where the FBI agent is and there are two scripts. One has the villain telling and the hero lets the villain go to jail and live, and in the other script, the villain refuses to tell and the hero blows the villain's fucking head off. Now let me give you your motivation. The FBI will be here any second, and they have to abide by the rules, but I don't. Tell me where Agent Lombardi is or I'll kill you."

Natty heard yells behind him, and, turning, he saw FBI agents in blue windbreakers and police officers flooding onto the scene, guns drawn. The lead agent ran over to Reed Forest and handed him a search warrant. He nodded at Tracker who was perturbed that the FBI had shown up so quickly. Reed Forest simply grinned.

Forest said to the lead agent, "I'm not saying anything to anybody without my attorney present."

The FBI agent looked at Reed Forest with hatred in his eyes and said through clenched teeth, "Where is Dominic Lombardi?"

Reed laughed and said, "Haven't seen him, officer."

The smiling actor looked over at Tracker and was surprised. The tall spy was putting on a pair of futuristic-looking sunglasses. He then walked around, his eyes scanning the house, outbuildings, and grounds. He walked over to the garden and Reed's eyes followed him.

Natty looked down where the FBI agent had been buried, and he immediately turned toward the lead agent and yelled, "He's buried right here and he's still alive!"

Excited, several agent ran over to the garden, but at the same time, several bodyguards panicked and whipped out automatic pistols and opened fire on the officers. One FBI agent and one Beverly Hills cop went down with bullets in their spines. Tracker pulled out his Glock 19 with the left hand and whipped out a lightweight Desert Eagle .44 Magnum semi-auto with his right. He stood upright and looked for armed bodyguards among the hysterically screaming party-goers and he fired at targets of opportunity with both pistols. Natty's eyes searched for Reed Forest but he was gone.

Reed and two of his bodyguards had already made their way through the escape tunnel under his walled estate, and he was now heading into his lover's house next door to borrow the man's white Lamborghini. The tunnel had been built by the previous owner after paranoid feelings arose after being blacklisted during the McCarthy days. It started in the fake back of the closet in the poolhouse, and the concrete pathway ran underground and exited at a trap door in the garden of the lover/neighbor next door. The damp tunnel had cracks and leaks from an earthquake, so the two men would never use it to go back and forth, but both knew about it.

The firing ended in minutes, and law enforcement officers started cuffing bodyguards left and right. Natty felt a pair of hands grab him from behind and toss him backward ten feet through the air. He lost both weapons because of the impact, but he did a breakfall when he hit the ground flat on his back. Unhurt, Tracker sprung to his feet and whirled to face his attacker. When Natty saw the size of the behemoth, he wished he hadn't looked.

It was July Jefferson, and Tracker thought back to some of the other monsters he had faced. Besides his finger laser, Tracker still had other weapons on him, but Natty always loved a challenge. Several officers ran up, weapons drawn. Grinning, Tracker signaled them away.

He and July squared off and closed in. July had never lost in his life, but Natty had and didn't like it at all. Tracker had faced bigger men than July and defeated them, but facing somebody bigger than himself was not something he really wanted to do. He especially was less than enthusiastic about facing a man with muscles the size of July Jefferson's.

The bigger man suddenly gave a roar and blitzed Natty, who struck him with a front foot defensive sidekick to the ribcage. The giant grunted and kept coming, but Tracker had already gotten out of the way. As the brute slipped past Natty, the handsome spy did a spinning hook kick to the back of his head and drove him face first into a marble birdbath. It scraped the skin off the big man's left cheek and jawline. Facial wounds bleed horribly and this was no exception. Within seconds, the left side of July's face was streaming blood. Natty struck the cheek twice in a second with two stinging backfists, faked a third, and shot out a hook kick to the face. It snapped the big man's head to the side. Tracker left his right foot up in the air and whipped it back into the bloody cheek with a vicious roundhouse kick that snapped the man's head the other way.

The giant's knees wobbled a little. He shook his mighty

head from side to side like a wounded grizzly, tucked it, and rushed in, his arms outspread. All his life, July Jefferson had grabbed many things, and he couldn't think of any of those things that didn't move when he got a hold of it. Natty Tracker was no exception. The monster swept Tracker up in a killer bearhug that trapped Natty's arms to his sides.

The man lifted Natty off the ground and squeezed with such brute strength that Tracker literally started seeing stars. The handsome superspy head-butted July on the right cheekbone, raising a big angry welt, and an angrier grin on the face of the Goliath. He tried two more head-butts, but watching for them, July slipped them both. Tracker then knee-smashed to the groin, but the big man had an insane look on his face and wouldn't let go even though he was in obvious pain. Tracker spit into the man's eyes three times in quick succession. He head-butted him again, and spit again, and followed with another head-butt that shattered the nose and sent blood spewing over both men's chests.

Natty then stepped back and side-kicked right to the base of the man's right kneecap, and he heard several women scream as the sickening snap of the giant knee echoed. The man went down, bounced back up on one leg, and swung a powerhouse right hook past Natty's head. Tracker slipped the punch, which could have killed any man if it had landed, and then he stepped in deep past the big man's left side and ridge-handed him full in the face with a tremendous right hand. The man's teeth flew backward and three of them went down his throat. Natty grabbed the hair on the back of July's head and jerked the brute's bloody head backward. With his lips curled back over his teeth, Tracker raised his powerful right arm up in the air and brought a shuto, or knife-hand strike down into the big man's windpipe, crushing it. July's eyes rolled back in his head while strangling sounds came out of his crushed throat. He fell back in the garden with flowers and leaves all around his head. His body kicked spasmodically, then died.

Natty dropped down where Dominic was buried and started digging with his hands. Other officers ran over while even more cops arrived and cuffed people left and right. The ones who joined Natty were warned by him to watch the garden hose sticking out of the ground. Tracker felt a foot and tickled it. It didn't move. They all dug frantically, and Tracker tickled the foot again and the toes wiggled. Several agents found shovels. Soon many cops and Tracker were on their knees or holding tools and were digging frantically in the rich soil.

Some cops even handcuffed prisoners to trees and joined in the digging. In no time, the naked agent was pulled from the soil and carried by Natty over to the swimming pool where he was dunked in the water and held like a baby. He laughed and then started crying. Tracker just held the naked federal cop while the man threw his arms around Natty's neck and cried his eyes out.

He kept saying between sobs over and over, "Thank you. Thank you, man, thank you so much."

An FBI agent came out of the house holding a towel he had secured and handed it to Natty. Natty and Dominic climbed out of the pool and Tracker handed the towel to Dom who started toweling off. It was a warm California night, but Lombardi shook like a tray of jello on a cheap vibrating bed. Cops and agents alike took turns walking over to the man and patting him on the back. Many also wanted to shake hands with Tracker, while behind his back one or two gathered here and there to tell some of the legendary stories about the super detective.

One cop was dead, an FBI agent paralyzed, another Beverly Hills officer had a bullet wound through the upper arm. Two bodyguards were dead, each body riddled with at least twenty bullets. Another had three bullet wounds and still another had suffered two wounds. A team of paramedics arrived and were taken immediately to Dominic

Lombardi, who insisted on going to headquarters to make out a report but was overruled by the lead agent.

Better than half of the LA membership of SAFE-PEACE was wearing nylon wristband cuffs and being placed into the back of a number of paddy wagons. In the meantime, Reed Forest and a number of his bodyguards had disappeared, along with the vice president and the secretary of the fanatical organization. Their Goliath, the behemoth July Jefferson, however, lay dead in a heap in the Beverly Hills garden.

The lead agent walked over to Natty Tracker while people were being ushered away by officers.

He said, "Mr. Tracker, how did you know that Agent Lombardi was buried there, and how did you know he was still alive?"

Natty smiled and said, "These glasses are called the OPTIC System. When I push this little button on the frame, I can see heat coming off of objects along with energy from the various colors and from electronic currents running in living beings. When I looked around, I could see a faint aura of color that outlined his body buried in the garden. I also could see little clouds of warm breath coming out of the end of the garden hose sticking out of the ground."

"I'll be damned," the G-man said. "Can I try them on?"

Natty grinned. "Sure, go ahead."

The agent tried them on and saw a jumble of colors and nothing else. He removed the glasses and handed them to a chuckling Natty.

Tracker said, "My eyes are equipped for them. Yours aren't."

The lead agent gave Natty a blank look and walked away scratching his head.

Tracker thought back to a beach in Libya, after his first infiltration. He had gotten headaches from his first OPTIC

System glasses and had taken them off to rest his eyes and head while waiting to be picked up for exfiltration.

Reaching into his duffel, Tracker pulled out a can of shaving cream and a disposable razor. He popped the dispenser off the can with his thumbnail and then screwed the bottom of the disposable razor into the top of the can. He pulled up on the razor, and it started spinning around like a miniature radar beacon. Natty then struck the side of the can with two hard pats, and a faint beeping sound came from within. He set the can down, and it continued to beep with the razor spinning above it emitting a continuous radio signal.

Natty lay down with his arms behind his head and closed his eyes. He then reached up and unplugged the two fiber optic leads hidden in his eyebrows. He removed the glasses, figuring that it would be a little while before transportation would arrive, homing in on his shaving-cream-and-razor transmitter.

Always on the alert since arriving in Libya, Natty was in need of some sleep. Within seconds, he was dreaming. The careful footsteps brought him fully awake, but because of prior training and experience, he did not move. He simply listened. There were two people and they had stopped. He knew that they must be shining a light on him and were only a few feet away. Tracker had figured out a way to give himself sight again and then had stupidly taken it away because his eyes were tired. To say that Natty was angry with himself would be an understatement.

Tracker tried to move but instantly froze at the sound of two guns being cocked right in front of him. His mind registered both sounds: one was a Swedish K while the other was a pistol. He knew that it was an automatic but couldn't figure out the model. He did know that regardless of the type or model, it could shoot holes in him.

The pistol barrel was shoved roughly under his chin while the holder grabbed his hair and pulled him to his feet, removing all chances of his replacing the OPTIC and

SOD Systems. Natty was now an unsighted man facing two armed enemies at a strange place where the sand meets the sea. It was hard to not panic, but panic was not Tracker's style.

A voice came out of the darkness, the pistol holder he thought, and the man said in broken English, "We knew when you watched the prison that we should follow with our lights out. You look like us. Are you Israeli?"

Tracker thought back to a particular karate class in which his instructor was teaching how to set up and counter a counter-puncher. The diminutive Korean master blindfolded himself and then had each student try to reverse-punch him full in the face or anywhere in the torso that they chose, provided that they wait until he moved first. Thus, each of them duplicated the actions of a counter-puncher. Natty remembered how he watched his instructor and was amazed as the man moved toward each opponent and brought his back hand up in front of him at hairline level and swept it downward with a dropping palm block. No matter where each adversary punched, the punch was caught by this technique and blocked harmlessly downward. Tracker had practiced this over and over and was surprised to find how easy it was to pick off a counter-puncher in this way. He felt that if he moved toward the speaker, the man would move the gun toward him to fire.

Being a man of decision, Natty stepped toward the speaker, bringing his right hand up in front of his face and sweeping it downward with a powerful palm block. At heart level, his block struck the hand with the gun in it. Natty stepped in close while his left hand closed around the other man's hand, squeezing the man's finger around the trigger guard so that it caused him to scream in pain.

In a millisecond, Tracker had deduced that the pistol holder probably held the flashlight, and that if he got in close, the other could not take a quick shot at him. He was right. Still trapping the pistol holder's hand around the butt, he stuck his own index finger through the trigger guard and swung the gun in the general direction of the rifle holder. Natty pulled the trigger as fast as his finger could move, and he tried to move the gun around while he fired off fourteen shots. He heard a body hit the ground but was still totally afraid for the first time in a long time. Was the man dropping to the ground to get a shot at him? Was he now aiming at Natty's heart? Was he just wounded and still capable of shooting Natty? Tracker just did not know.

The speaker had no choice in the shooting as he was in extreme pain from Natty's wrist-lock and finger-squeeze on him. Tracker forced the now-empty pistol back into the screaming man's open mouth and swung viciously upward with a left elbow smash that caught the man under the chin and broke all his teeth on the gun barrel. Quickly, Natty reached down with his left hand, grabbed the man's groin, then squeezed and twisted it violently. He then punched him in the face while still holding the pistol. The butt of the automatic demolished the man's facial bones as Natty struck him with all of his might, which was a lot of might considering that Natty could bench-press 375 pounds.

Next, Natty dropped to the ground and did a somersault with his heels coming down hard where he figured the rifle-holder's chest would be. Tracker's feet hit sand, and he froze as he heard the man chuckle weakly, death in his voice, both his own and Tracker's. The man sounded like he was about ten feet away. Tracker stood as the man continued to chuckle. Natty faced the rifleman and knew by the man's dying laugh that he had no chance.

In very thick English, the rifleman said, "Israeli?"

Tracker stuck his jaw out defiantly, gave the man the finger, and said, "Fuck you!"

Whoosh! Thunk! Wham! The sounds came almost simultaneously, and Tracker was on the ground crawling. His hand touched his glasses, and he quickly pulled them on and plugged them in. He also inserted his sonar ear piece. Sweat poured down his face as he took in the scene in front of him. The man who had held the pistol was lying on the ground with his face hideously caved in and was very dead. The rifleman lay beyond him on his back with a spearfishing harpoon protruding from his forehead. He weighed close to 250 pounds, Tracker estimated, and appeared to have bullet holes in his neck, chest, left hip, and lower right abdomen. This had been one tough sucker, and Natty was thankful that he didn't have to fight him hand to hand. On the beach to Tracker's right stood two U.S. Navy SEAL's in scuba gear and wet suits.

The one holding the speargun said, "Wonder . . ."

And Natty replied, "Woman . . . has big tits."

The SEAL laughed, "Howdy, you were only supposed to respond with the word 'woman.' "

Tracker replied, "Hey, did you ever look at Wonder Woman?"

The SEAL laughed, "Yeah, I see what you mean. Mother fuck, look what you did to that guy's face, mister."

Tracker responded, "Well, I was one dead son of a bitch. I can't tell you how glad I am that you guys showed up. Thanks."

"Aw shit, our pleasure," the seal said modestly. "I'm just glad we got some action since our little raft and us had to swim out of a submarine's torpedo tubes to get here. Made me feel like I was a giant sperm cell. Which reminds me. This is Libya. Why don't we just jump in our rubber boat and get the fuck out of here?"

"We can't yet. These bodies cannot be found," Natty said. "We have got to get rid of the bodies and sterilize the area."

"No sweat," the SEAL said with his cheerful gravelly voice.

He and his partner ran forward and each swept up a body over his shoulders and quickly kicked sand over the blood and footprints. One tossed Tracker's bag to him which he caught, as he thought a silent "thank you" for his SOD and OPTIC Systems. They jumped in the raft with the bodies and were joined by Tracker who pushed the rubber craft out into the mild surf. They started rowing and the leader laughed in Natty's direction.

He said, "Hey, ah, it's 0400 hours. You can take off yer Foster Grants, you know."

Tracker smiled and yelled above the sound of the waves, "Can't help it. When you guys saved my bacon back there, you just dazzled me with your brilliance. Shhh!"

Tracker whispered, "Don't move; a boat's coming."

The head SEAL whispered carefully, "Probably the sub. No sweat."

Natty replied, "No, the sub is still submerged about a mile farther out. This one's going to be coming around that bend. Lay down in the raft."

A minute later, a Libyan patrol boat came around the shore and passed by, its spotlight passing above the bobbing black raft.

After it passed, the two SEALS rowed faster as the leader spoke again, "Fuck, was that close. How in the hell did you hear that boat? And how in the hell did you know where the sub is?"

Tracker smiled, "It's simple: I'm just wearing sunglasses to cut down the bright moonlight and starlight. If you guys would wear them, you would've seen both boats, too. As a matter of fact, the sub is near the surface now."

Both SEALS turned and a minute later saw the large nuclear sub silently break the water's surface.

The previously silent SEAL finally spoke to the leader, "I finally figured it out, Lieutenant. He's Spiderman."

Tracker thought about how incredible some of his inventions were and how they would revolutionize law enforcement and intelligence gathering as well as aid the visually impaired. It amazed Natty that he had actually figured out a practical way for an unsighted person to see.

He couldn't wait until his inventions were made public and were no longer in the experimental phase.

It was going to take all of his inventions now to locate and capture or kill Reed Forest. Natty knew one thing. The man hadn't became a major motion picture star without having at least some acting ability, if not a lot. He was one of the most recognizable people in the world, so he definitely would have to get into disguise immediately. He also was very wealthy and had wealthy friends. The man could be hiding anywhere in the world and would probably be able to pull off just about any kind of charade that he wanted to. He also would want Natty Tracker dead a lot more now than ever before. Reed Forest had to know that Tracker would come after him with a vengeance. The question of the hour was: How the hell was Natty going to find him?

5.

A Cry in the Sky

NATTY TRACKER HARDLY ever flew on commercial aircraft. In fact, when he flew out to Los Angeles to meet with the FBI agent who had gone undercover in the SAFE-PEACE organization, he had packed up his Hovercopter in its special pod under his F-15E Eagle. Unfortunately, on his flight to Los Angeles, Tracker had some problems with the FLIR, the Forward Looking Infrared. He had to leave the jet there to be worked on by Air Force personnel with the proper security clearance, and he booked himself on a flight to Denver's Stapleton International Airport. Natty could have had his assistant and copilot, a retired Air America pilot, pick him up, but instead he called Dee Light and asked her to pick him up. Natty remembered that she was taking some leave and was visiting her mother in Colorado. Then she was going to spend a few days with him if he was in town. She was delighted to pick him up.

After storing his Hovercopter back in its pod under the jet, Natty got an FBI ride to LAX and checked in. The smog was thick when the 727 jet took off and swung out through the off-white thick air over the blue waters of the Pacific. Two teenagers surfing by the short pier at Playa del Ray heard the mighty jet engines roar as it launched off the end of the runway and climbed out and up over the ocean, but they could only hear the roar of the engines, not see the aircraft. It climbed and turned in a big circle and headed toward Denver.

Bradley Renninger was a FAC, a Forward Air Controller, in South Vietnam. When ground troops got into a firefight with North Vietnamese soldiers or the Viet Cong, the commander, wanting to call in an air strike, could not speak directly to the jet fighters. Instead, he spoke to a FAC. The FAC, an Air Force officer, usually flying a single-engine O-1 or L-19 aircraft equipped with a few rockets and little else, flew over and communicated with the ground commander. He called in jets on a different radio and then had the ground pounder mark his spot and direct him to the enemy location. The FAC, usually exposing himself to the enemy unit's fire, then fired a rocket into the enemy position to mark it. The white phosphorous rocket gave off a long continuous cloud of billowy white smoke and gave the jets a good target to drop their ordnance on. More than one FAC was shot down in Vietnam; in fact, it was the rule, not the exception.

Brad was no different. He left the "Big Rifle Range Across the Pond" with a fistful of air medals, a couple of purple hearts, and a mind full of memories, some bad and some good. He also had become a "head." Bored with off-duty nights sitting around the O-club getting drunk, he got talked into trying some Laotian grass one night. The first time he smoked it, it felt like somebody had placed a giant leather belt around his forehead and made a tourniquet out of it. It kept tightening and tightening, and his eyebrows felt like they were elevated to his hairline. The next time, he was tripping on the powerful weed. After that, he got stoned every chance he could, and unlike others, he made his joints by emptying out Marlboro cigarettes by rolling the white part between his fingers and letting the tobacco fall out. He then tamped the pot in and twisted the end. This helped ease the raw burning pain the powerful grass caused in his throat.

After Vietnam, he went back to his first love, jets, and flew B-52s and C-141s. After his retirement in 1982, he went to work as a commercial airline pilot and was introduced to coke by a sweet little blond flight attendant who provided him with blow. The coke made his grass highs seem like caffeine in comparison, and Bradley started the downhill slide to heavy duty addiction.

It kept getting worse and worse until the fateful day that Natty Tracker flew on Bradley's flight to Denver. That was the day Bradley lost count of how many lines of blow he had done. The blue-uniformed, gray-haired man was flying long before he arrived at the LAX.

The flight was uneventful until the jet got near the border between Utah and Colorado. That's when all the lines of Colombian snow, all the cans of beer, all the greasy hamburgers, bowls of ice cream, and soft chairs caught up with Bradley Renninger. His heart exploded, and his eyes rolled up in his head as he gave out a loud cry of pain. He jumped up slightly and started to fall over the controls of the big jet. His copilot, totally startled, jumped up immediately and tried to grab Brad. Brad's weight, suddenly falling and totally limp in death, pulled the man down quickly and he slammed his head on the instrument panel and fell, unconscious, across the dead body of Bradley Renninger. The navigator almost wet his pants and tried to pull the two slumped bodies away from the forward part of the engine compartment. This, unfortunately, was the third part of the strange coincidence. The navigator was a great guy, but he weighed about one hundred and twenty-eight pounds soaking wet while holding a pound of butter. If he had ever tried to lift weights, he would have found that he was unable to bench press even one hundred pounds. Both the late Brad Renninger and the comatose copilot weighed well over two hundred pounds each.

When the pilot died and fell on the controls, the jet suddenly dropped in altitude and some of the passengers cried out. Natty knew that it was not turbulence, and all of his senses came on the alert. He watched and waited. A few seconds later, the head flight attendant entered the cockpit and came out a minute later with an ashen look on her face. Natty could see past the forced smile and watched as she gave flyers phony grins and gathered up the other flight attendants and whispered brief statements to each. A voice different from the pilot's came over the PA system and assured everyone that some turbulence had just been experienced and that was the reason for the change in altitude.

Tracker had seen and heard enough, so he got up and walked directly toward the cockpit door. The head flight attendant ran forward, caught him by the arm, and couldn't help but notice the bulging muscles.

"Sir, you can't go in there," she said, trying to sound calm and forceful.

Natty smiled and stared into her eyes and said very softly, "Ma'am, I'm a pilot and can probably get us down on the ground safely if there isn't a pilot up there. I have a feeling that there isn't. Something happened. Tell me, am I wrong?"

She stared into his light blue eyes and saw strength, a quiet strength that made her feel safe, even in this emergency.

She looked around at the other passengers, some not noticing what had been happening, others with worried looks on their faces.

She whispered softly, "Please, sir, come with me. The pilot's dead and the copilot's dead or unconscious."

A few minutes later, the pilot's body and the limp copilot were laid out behind the two padded flight seats. Tracker was seated in the pilot's spot and was talking to the tower at Stapleton International.

A commanding and friendly voice came over the radio and said, "Okay, Mr. Tracker, what have you flown?"

Natty said, "Twin- and single-engine and rotary, and in jets, Lear, F-15, F-16, F-14 once, and the Aardvark."

The voice laughed and said, "Can you imagine driving a Corvette all around and then me telling you how to drive a Rolls Royce Silver Shadow? That's what it's going to be like for you to fly this baby home and land it. It almost flies itself."

Tracker brought the big jet in beautifully, listening to the commands of the man in the control tower. Tracker learned that the man was an executive for United but had been a pilot for many years. There were ambulances and emergency vehicles all over the runway when he brought the big bird down. The landing, however, was smooth and trouble free. When Natty taxied the plane down the tarmac, it looked like half of Denver was there to greet the plane. All the news media were definitely there.

Finally, the big jet came to a halt, and stairs were wheeled up to it. People flooded onto the plane, and the passengers flooded off. The medical personnel strapped the still unconscious copilot onto a backboard and transferred him to a stretcher and took him away. Another ambulance took away the body of the dead pilot, and then Natty and the crew left the jet. Reporters and photographers flooded around Natty, and beyond them, he saw a very beautiful, brightly smiling Secret Service agent named Dee Light. He started walking toward her, ignoring reporters and their questions.

A news cameraman stuck a Sony Beta SP camera in his face while a pretty female reporter shoved a microphone under his nose and said, "Sir, are you the man who took over control of the jet when the pilot died and the copilot got hurt?"

Natty looked away from Dee and gave the reporter a curious look. He then noticed an older gentleman from the plane who had been quite a bit in his cups before boarding, and Natty had seen him pull a flask out of his suit coat several times during the the flight and imbibe. He pointed at the man with his thumb and smiled.

"No," Tracker replied. "It was him."

The lady looked shocked, but then she and the cameraman dashed over to the inebriated businessman and started asking questions. Other reporters, seeing this, flooded past Natty and surrounded the drunk. He and Dee laughed heartily, greeted each other with a big hug and kiss, and sped down the hallway holding hands.

"Can't you just fly a plane from point A to point B without being a superhero?" Dee asked.

Natty smiled and said, "Honey, I'm sorry, but I was just doing what I do best."

"What's that?" she said.

"Showing off."

As they walked on away from the crowd and the *paparrazzi* Natty said, "Remember when the hero crap really started?"

Dee smiled, "Remember, how could I forget? Besides, it isn't crap. That's for sure."

They walked along and waited for Natty's luggage, both recalling in their minds the major incident involving them both that had made him legendary.

He and Dee had been at his ranch property riding their horses and had been trying to take some time off from work. At the time, Tracker did not know that Dee was a Secret Service agent assigned to watch over him by no less than the President of the United States. Even Wally Rampart didn't know that she was Secret Service, mainly because the few times that he had been around when she was guarding the President, Vice President, or others, her long beautiful red hair had been up in a bun or French twist, and she had worn sunglasses. On top of that, it was her job to go unnoticed. That task in itself was a monumental one for a lady with the body and looks of Dee

Light. At the time, Natty and Wally Rampart both had been led to believe that the beauty was a Colorado Springs copyright/patent attorney. Not long afterward, she had occasion to save Natty's life and then let him know her true work.

The afternoon that his legend took the giant stride started with a wonderful love-making session with Dee and Tracker in a small patch of woods. The secluded meadows through which they rode were dotted with small two- to five-acre stands of trees. Leading the way, Dee rode into one of these little groves and halted her mount. She got down and gave Tracker a cute, impish smile.

"Nature calls," she said as she walked in amongst the trees and out of sight.

Natty sat on his horse and studied the beauty about him. A little mountain bluebird landed on a branch near his head.

It seemed to study the big non-threatening animal as he said to it, "Why is it, little bluebird, that we humans have to invest in stocks and bonds, open savings accounts, and buy CDs to provide for our futures? You just trust in God, and every day of your life, you awaken and go out and you are provided with the food and shelter that you need. I wonder if you and your brothers and sisters ever get ulcers or strokes worrying about your food each day. Somehow, I think that you don't."

Natty looked around, wondering what was taking Dee so long.

He looked up at the cumulus cloud formations in the clear blue sky. The elevation here was 7,900 feet, and at night, the entire sky looked like a giant black drape with billions of glittering diamonds dotting every square inch. You could stand in the meadow where Natty and Dee now were and see a meteor every few seconds.

Tracker chuckled and spoke to the little bird again, "On the other hand, I guess we don't go around eating worms all day long."

"Oh, I don't know," Dee's voice came from behind Natty.

Grinning, he turned and gave a long slow whistle. Dee was wearing her vest, hat, scarf, spurs, and chaps. Missing were her shirt, Levis, boots, and socks. Natty stared at one nipple peeking out from the vest and then down at the sparse triangle of red pubic hair outlined by the tops of her chaps.

She grinned seductively and said, "Hey, cowboy, wanna try a little bronc bustin'?"

Tracker dismounted and walked toward her with a nasty smile on his handsome face and an impish twinkle in his baby-blues.

He said, "I don't like to bust broncs, I like to gentle them."

She laughed and responded, "Wanna ride bareback?"

"Are you going to use those spurs?"

"If you're lucky," she purred.

He swept her into his powerful arms and their lips came together with smoldering passion. He laid her gently in the grass and they came together.

Two hours later, Natty awakened and looked at Dee's beautiful face cradled on his left bicep. He softly kissed her forehead and a smile spread across her lips. Tracker stood and started putting his clothing back on. She yawned and stretched while Natty stared at her full breasts and felt a heat stirring his loins again. He decided to torture himself and wait until later. She stood up and dressed. Fully clothed, they came together, kissed long and hard, and then mounted their horses after replacing their bridles and bits.

"Let's ride down through Spike Buck Gulch," Natty said. "It's a beautiful ride."

"Where does it come out?" she asked.

"At the Five Points rest area on Highway 50," he replied. "By the time we get there, a lot of bighorn sheep will be coming down to the Arkansas to drink. You can get some great pictures. A lot of times two rams get into a head-butting contest.''

"Oh, Natty, I'd love to get that on film," Dee replied. "Let's ride."

They trotted out of the trees and pulled up immediately. A group of ten rough-looking horsemen, all in cowboy attire, galloped across the meadow toward them and were only fifty yards off. Natty quickly squinted his left eye and zoomed in on the men to check out their armament. He stuck the EAR device in his right ear and listened to the two in the center who were talking.

One said, "We kill him first and then fuck the woman and kill her, too."

"Awright!" the other yelled enthusiastically.

Natty said, "Honey, they plan to kill us both. Ride like the wind to Five Points and don't stop. Flag down a car."

"But Natty—" she started to protest.

Tracker slapped her horse on the rump and yelled, *"Go!"*

The horse shot back through the patch of trees like lightning. Four of the approaching riders spurred their horses into action, but Natty's revolver cleared leather and boomed. Sighting down the barrel with his eyesight zoomed in, he took the first horse through the head, although he had aimed for the rider. The second horse tripped and somersaulted over the falling horse and rider. Tracker shot again and the third rider spilled out of the saddle. The fourth reined up and bolted his horse over to his six breathing comrades.

The leader held his hand high in the air. Natty was suspicious; just then, he heard several guns cock behind him. He slowly replaced his gun in the leather holster and raised his hands.

The leader reined up in front of Natty and grinned. He was riding a large blood bay and was dressed like a cowboy, with the exception of a dirty baseball cap with a Caterpillar tractor logo on the front. The big man pulled a

Browning Hi-power nine millimeter semi-automatic from a shoulder holster.

In the eighteen hundreds, Streeter and Tom McCoy held up trains along the Arkansas River and then escaped by coming up through the narrows of Spike Buck Gulch, where Natty had just sent Dee. They also were occasionally questioned about their creative artwork on cattle brands in the area, as well as unauthorized and rather violent withdrawals from local banks from Salida to Canon City.

The pair and their gang became such a problem in the area that the famous lawman Tom Horn was finally imported to nearby Cotopaxi to bring the duo and their cohorts to justice.

One of those bandits who ran with the McCoys was a sometime puncher, sometime outlaw, named Bandy Williams. He fathered a boy named Buck who was hanged for rape and murder, but not before his son Tim was born. Tim also died of ''hemp fever'' for altering a few too many brands, but only after he fathered a son named Lou, who begat a son named Buck, after his infamous ancestor. Lou died of syphilis in a federal penitentiary, and Buck now sat on a big rawboned blood bay gelding and was pointing a pistol at Natty Tracker. Somebody came up from behind and pulled Natty's .44 out of his holster.

Buck claimed to be a local big game guide and outfitter and surrounded himself with other rough-looking punchers who all loved the bottle. For the most part, Buck's gang did a bit of drinking and hell-raising, but they did gang-rape a woman one night near Pueblo, and they were hired by a very racially prejudiced rancher to kill a black man who had bought the adjoining ranch. They did so and enjoyed the job a little too much. The gang thirsted for blood, and seeing the beautiful Dee Light as a fringe benefit, made it almost worth doing for free in their minds.

Tracker heard more horses riding up behind him and turned his head. Three horses rode up with two more outlaws on each side of Dee holding her arms. Tears streaked down her face. Several outlaws chuckled evilly, and she was immediately pulled off of her horse and her clothes were torn off her body. She screamed and was slapped across the face.

Dee gave Natty a pleading look, but he remained expressionless. Tracker had had to watch while his love, Dr. Fancy Bird, was raped and sodomized by the notorious international terrorist called The Ratel. Tracker got hysterical and just about lost it then, thus rendering himself helpless. He decided right then, if ever in that position again, he would remain as cool as a cucumber, so he could think his way out of the problem.

"Kill him and let's have at her," Buck commanded.

Several men aimed at Natty, but his words stopped them.

"Wait!" Natty said.

Buck held up his hand and said, "Why? I reckon yer jus' tryin' to save yer fuckin' neck, huh?"

Tracker said, "No, I'm dead, and I know that you're going to kill her, too. I'm just trying to keep her from being raped first."

Natty stared into the man's eyes. He chanced pretending to scratch behind his ear and activated the video recorder. A gesture warned him to get his hand back up. His mind raced for ways to try to stall and hope that somebody was monitoring Wally Rampart's computer screen. Staring at Buck made Buck uneasy and wonder if the guy was really being honest.

"Go on," Buck said.

"Look," Natty said very earnestly, "ask anybody that knows me. I never lie, no matter what. She and I are lovers because we both have herpes."

"Bullshit," Buck said. "Nice try. Kill him."

"I can prove it," Natty said. "Easy."

"How?" Buck asked, really starting to wonder.

Natty replied, "The only thing I have to gain is you guys not raping her. I know you're going to kill us. I have herpes sores on my organ. Let me get down real slowly and carefully, and I'll show you. No tricks. You have my word.''

Buck laughed, ''Aw, what the fuck! Well, you dismount real slow and pull out your dick there, an' we'll take a look-see. Any tricks an' ya' both die slow, 'stead of fast. Comprendez?''

Natty pretended to shake, which wasn't that difficult, as he realized that Wally couldn't save him here that quickly, even if he was watching the action. Tracker slowly dismounted.

''Can I ask why you're going to kill me?'' Natty said as he slowly got to the ground.

''Sure,'' Buck said. ''Some attorney name of Ralph Wendell hired me to. Drop them drawers.''

Natty slowly unzipped his pants and reached down in his underwear.

He grinned sheepishly at Buck and said, ''I lied!'' as he put his first nine millimeter round right between the man's eyes.

His left hand went up behind his back as he spun on his heels, and his arm whipped out with a vicious throw of a dagger that had been sheathed between his shoulder blades. The blade buried itself in the left cheek of an outlaw who had already dropped his jeans and was trying to get between Dee's legs.

Tracker's hideout gun spouted flames as he fired bullets into the bodies of the three men holding her down. Bullets struck where Tracker had been, but he was already somersaulting and firing the lightweight Glock 19 nine millimeter automatic. Natty knew that he could not miss with one shot, and he scored with all eighteen rounds. They spurted out of the small gun almost as fast as a machinegun.

When the gun came up empty, one tough-looking puncher still stood, and he grinned at Natty as he walked forward, a cocky look on his scarred face. He gestured with the sawed-off twelve gauge shotgun he was carrying, and Natty grinned at him and hooked his thumbs in the front of his belt by the buckle, an antique western sheriff's star.

"Guess I should have saved one bullet, huh?" Tracker said.

"Guess so," the killer said with a grin. "Good shootin', though."

He glanced at the dagger sticking out of the one dead man's face and said, "Nice throw too, boy."

Tracker grinned broadly and said, "Wanna see it again?"

The man got a puzzled look on his face. Suddenly, Natty's right hand whipped out from the belt buckle, and something flew rapidly through the air with a whoosh. The shotgunner's eyes crossed and rolled up, looking as if he were trying to stare at the blades sticking out of his forehead. The heavy belt buckle was not really a sheriff's star, but was actually a shuriken, the deadly six-pointed throwing star knives made famous by the old Japanese ninja assassins. Tracker had dived to his right with the throw while his left hand pulled a second Glock 19 from his left boot. Natty put four rounds into the killer before his body hit the ground.

Dee jumped up, and Tracker commanded, "Stay down."

He jumped up and quickly covered each downed man with his pistol, both hands on the grip, arms outstretched. He went from one to the next and checked the pulse of each. He found three who were still breathing, and he quickly dispatched each with a round in the forehead.

As Tracker got close to the small stand of trees, a big outlaw on a dirty palomino gelding spurred his horse out of the trees and rammed it chest first into Natty. The man took off across the pasture at a dead run as Tracker, losing his gun, flew through the air and hit the ground in a ball, somersaulting into a spring for his own horse, Eagle.

Tracker vaulted into the saddle with a leap over the horse's rump. Natty and Eagle blazed across the meadow and through another stand of trees that cut short the course the outlaw took down the old mining road. Tracker came out of the trees in a dizzying lope about twenty yards behind the bad guy. In a few minutes, Eagle easily overtook the other horse and pulled up alongside. Natty leaped sideways through the air, his left arm closing around the man's windpipe and his left hand wrapped around the base of his right bicep while the right arm went up across the back of the crook's head. He squeezed hard as they flew out of the saddle. Tracker saw the ground rushing at him, and he tightened his diaphragm and tightened his grip on the man's head and neck. They hit and there was a loud snapping noise as the criminal's neck broke in two places. It took Natty fifteen minutes to catch both horses and sling the body over the saddle and return to Dee.

He unloaded the body and walked over to the beautiful attorney and crossed his arms.

"Okay, honey," Tracker said softly, "you're safe."

She jumped up and ran to him, throwing her arms around his neck and started sobbing heavily. He held her and stroked her red tresses while she sobbed hysterically in his strong arms. She tried to walk to her clothes, and her knees buckled. Natty caught her, lifted her up, and carried her over into the shade.

He laid her down on the mountain gramma grass and several clumps of loco weed. Next, he ran to a dead horse, stripped the saddle off, and carried it to Dee. He laid it down and set both her feet on top of it, elevating her legs to get blood to her head. After three minutes, she could stand up but then started vomiting. Tracker got her a canteen, and she drank the entire contents. Natty didn't move her for a full hour and made her lie there to catch her wits.

He turned the video recorder mode for his eyes off until she got dressed again, then he went to each body with the recorder going and checked the identification. He also held up each corpse's finger in front of one eye and zoomed his vision in so there would be fingerprint identification on each one.

Tracker finished his inspection work and surveyed the carnage he had wrought. He knew, in spite of himself, that a new Tracker legend had been born and would be repeated and exaggerated all over Capitol Hill and in intelligence circles all over the world.

The property was so out of the way that it would be a simple matter for the government to hush up the killings. Tracker looked at the bodies. He had been confronted by armed men who had the drop on him, and he had killed them all with three pistols, one knife, and one shuriken. Sixteen bodies lay on the bloody ground in front of him.

Natty had built a campfire and made trail coffee. He walked over to the fire and Dee handed him a cup. A woman of incredible strength, she smiled and was effectively dealing with the ordeal. Tracker made her promise to see a counselor, however, and she agreed to do so. He also promised her a luxury month-long vacation by herself, anywhere in the world she wanted to go. She didn't argue and told him Paris would be wonderful.

"Are we okay here?" she asked.

"Yeah," he replied. "People will show up shortly, tons of them."

"But how, Natty?" Dee asked. "We haven't called anybody or sent any kind of signals."

Natty laughed and said, "Trust me. They'll be here."

"Natty, you saved my life," she said, "but I'm an officer of the court, and you shot three of them dead. I feel strange. I mean, I know that they wanted to kill me . . ."

Natty held up his finger and shushed her. "I understand. Honey, I'm allowed to kill people. It's exactly like a war situation."

"You are allowed?" she asked. "I won't ask any more questions. I know that you are very, very powerful in Washington. I'm just glad that you're on our side."

Tracker smiled and kissed her. He held her tightly and stared at the flames of the fire while she cried softly against his chest.

Suddenly, Tracker heard the drone of a single-engine plane overhead and looked up when he heard it stall. Spotting it, he zoomed his eyesight in and saw a skydiver exiting the door of the Cessna. The man had a black jumpsuit on and had what looked to be an M-16 rifle attached to his webbing. Tracker sent Dee into the trees, and he pulled out one Glock 19 and his .44 Magnum.

Because they were so out of the way, Dee had mistakenly left her weaponry in a bag in Tracker's car, thinking that they were out of harm's way. Professionally, she was ashamed of herself for the gross oversight, but of course couldn't share her thoughts with her unknowing lover. The President had made it clear that Tracker did have an ego and might resent him assigning her to him for additional protection. He also made it clear that it was okay with him if she got involved with Natty, just so long as she could help keep him safe. She had considered this outing as a day off, but she vowed she would never be around Natty again without her weapon and backup gun. If she ever had to shoot to protect him, Dee would then let him know her true job and mission, but until then, he really didn't need to know.

The goggled skydiver tracked toward Natty's fire and shifted into a frog position. He deployed his black Para-commander chute at about 1,500 feet and got his M-16 ready to fire. A few minutes later, the man hit the ground and literally ran out of his harness, heading toward Tracker's fire. Three fast shots kicked dirt up under his feet, and Natty's voice from behind a lone tree stopped him short.

"Drop the rifle and eat the ground fast! Don't talk! Don't move!" Tracker yelled.

The man dropped his M-16 immediately and hit the

ground in a spread-eagle position. Tracker ran over to him and pointed the cocked Glock 19 at him.

"Remove the goggles and roll over slowly," Natty commanded.

"Son of a bitch!" Natty said as he looked down into the grinning walrus-mustachioed face of Undersecretary of State Wally Rampart.

Tracker gave him a hand and helped him dust off the jumpsuit.

"What the fuck?" Natty said.

"Hell, Tracker," the old warhorse bellowed, "I come to save your bacon, and you kill all the bad guys before I even get here."

Natty, dumfounded, walked him over to the coffee pot as Dee ran out of the woods grinning and threw her arms around Wally's neck giving him a big hug and kiss on the cheek.

Wally took a long sip of coffee and the other two followed suit.

"What the—why are you here, General?" Natty asked.

The old general said, "What am I doing here? I was flying this way to locate you and drop you a message. I got a call about you being in trouble, and the plane had jump gear in it, so here I am."

"Why did you fly out here to give me a message?" Natty asked.

" 'Cause you have every communication system we use shut down, you dumb son of a bitch. Why else?"

Tracker grinned.

He sipped his coffee and said, "Sorry, General, I do need some time to myself, you know."

Wally grumbled, "Yeah, well what if the President needed you for some mission right away?"

Dee stared back and forth at the two men. She had to act like she didn't know exactly what Tracker did, so when the words "the President" came out in the conversation, she gasped.

The old general lit up a Havana cigar after offering one to Natty while he scowled at the handsome spy.

Natty replied, "I guess the President would just have to wait, wouldn't he?"

"Dammit, you don't make the President of the United States wait while you're out in the woods playing kissy-face with a beautiful woman!" Wally roared.

He cleared his throat and said softly, "No offense, Miss Light."

Dee laughed heartily. "On the contrary; I took that as a compliment."

Tracker started laughing and said, "Why, is the President jealous, because he watched your monitor and got to see Dee with her clothes off?"

Dee jumped up, red-faced, and yelled, "What monitor? Natty, have you videotaped us . . . I mean . . . have you . . . Oh!"

Tracker jumped up and softly grabbed her arms and tried to explain. This time it was Wally's turn to laugh heartily while Natty tried to squirm out of this one. Dee pulled away from the half-breed.

"Dee, listen to me," he said, "I never videotaped you in the nude. Well, not intentionally, but . . ."

"Not intentionally!" she screamed. "Well, how many damned people did you show your porno tapes to? The ones that you *accidentally* took of me!"

Natty grabbed her arms again, and she jerked herself out of his copper hands and stormed off through the trees. Tracker followed after her pleading all the way. In the meantime, Wally Rampart held his sides and howled with laughter and literally fell over backward off the log. He lay on the ground while the red-faced master sleuth tried to talk his way out of his predicament.

In a few minutes, they came back with Dee still fuming and Wally still laughing. Both sat down on opposite ends of the log, and grinning, the old general handed each a cup of coffee.

"Oh, by the way, Tracker," Wally said with a mischievous grin, "the signal that showed Dee's nudity got mixed up with the NBC satellite, and it went out over the airwaves during the 'Oprah Winfrey Show.' "

Dee drew in a breath, stood, and slapped Natty across the face while Wally again fell off of the log in hysterical laughter.

"Thanks a lot," Tracker snapped at the general as he again followed Dee into the little patch of woods.

Natty turned to follow her and stepped right into a sapling, tripped as he tried to adjust his balance, and fell on the ground. Dee happened to be looking and saw this and saw the old general laughing even harder, so she started laughing. Tracker picked himself up and dusted off his clothes. His face was totally red, and he was almost shaking with rage and embarrassment. The whole situation suddenly struck his funny bone, and he started laughing at himself.

The three sat on the log and laughed and shared some more coffee, then Natty explained to Dee about his eyes and his inventions. She knew something about him, as the President had given her a file on Tracker, but she didn't know everything. Nevertheless, she had to play dumb anyway. The Undersecretary let her know that he hadn't seen her and doubted if anybody other than his female secretary had. He also assured her that the tapes would be edited to conceal her nudity and identity.

Helicopters, ordered by Wally Rampart, started filling the sky and the meadow. Soldiers poured out. The area was cleaned up and the bodies removed. Several FBI agents arrived with the Army, and they talked to Natty and Dee. One took the keys to Tracker's car and volunteered to drive it back to Colorado Springs, while Tracker, Dee, and Wally rode back in an Army helicopter after Dee got her bag from the car which held her two guns.

An hour later, the trio sat in Tracker's study at the base of Cheyenne Mountain. A glass of iced tea in his hand,

Natty looked out the window at the Will Rogers Memorial Statue near the Cheyenne Mountain Zoo. Beyond the statue, at about 14,000 feet, thick billowy, white clouds smothered the top of majestic Pike's Peak and kept it from looking out at the endless miles of prairie to the east and the purple mountains to the north, west, and south.

Now Tracker wondered if he would again beat the odds and be successful again. Could he and would he find and kill or capture Reed Forest and his cohorts? Would he do it before they killed more innocent people in the name of peace, love, and conservation? Any man who would bury an FBI agent upside down, alive, with an air hose so he'd suffer longer had to be one sick, ruthless, cold son of a bitch, Natty thought. He decided that he had better be very careful or he might end up buried himself.

6.

Hide and Seek

COON MORGAN WAS originally employed by James Earl Smith, the megapunk crooked billionaire, who was dethroned and killed by Natty Tracker. It was an incredible coincidence that he would be completing a circle now and coming back into Tracker's life in a roundabout way. Morgan had reinvested some of the money he made from Smith's scam. He had invested it in Peruvian blow, part of which went up his nose. More and more snow kept going up that worn double passageway, so even the money he made by buying and selling more coke was almost gone. That's why he left southern Mexico to look for work, big money work.

He didn't know that his employer was actually the famous movie star Reed Forest, who had disappeared. Coon had been hired by a middle man. The middle man, however, like everyone else, didn't know Coon by that name. Everybody knew him by the name he had gotten from the judge. The name that made him some heavy duty bread, Robert Greenfield. Robert had gotten the name Coon in the joint, but he didn't have the only unusual name there.

Badass Rivers lived up to his name. He was serving three consecutive life sentences in the Ohio State Penitentiary for three very gruesome murders and several counts of rape. He was six feet seven and about two hundred and fifty pounds in the ninth grade, so he learned early to become a vicious bully. Various knife and bullet scars crisscrossed his pasty-white body. An abused child, he had been in and out of juvenile detention and had spent most of his adult life in prison. Even there, he was very intimidating to most convicts, and he took from them what he wanted, whenever he wanted. Prisoners, however, have certain ways of dealing with people.

Badass was lying across his bunk in tier three. Fast asleep, he never saw the five inmates who sneaked into his cell led by a five-foot-four-inch short-timer named Coon Morgan. Coon was nobody's bitch. He had survived five years in the pen and twenty-five years in the ghetto by using his wits and had only three days to go, but Badass had taken a pack of cigarettes from him the day before.

While several inmates watched for approaching guards, the other four slipped a blanket over Badass' entire body and held the sides of the blanket tightly down. He could not budge in any direction because he was tightly trapped against the cot by the olive blanket. The pillowcases from the top and bottom bunks were used by Coon to tie the man's ankles to the bunkbed's frame. Coon pulled the struggling giant's trousers down and got on top of his back. He brutally sodomized the man, and the other four took turns raping him also. The giant tried to scream during the attack, but his face was shoved into his pillow.

After the last rapist climaxed, Coon leaned down and spoke through the blanket into Badass' ear, "Yo' Badass, you my bitch now. You fuck wid a truck, you get yo' young ass run over. Any my brothers want you to suck dere mothah fuckin' dicks, you gonna do it. Unnerstan'?"

Crying beneath the blanket for the first time since infancy, Badass weakly nodded his head affirmatively.

Coon went on, "Yo' fuckin' name no longer be Badass, man. From now on yo' name be Bloodyass. You fuck wid any brothers in this fuckin' place ever again, next time a shiv be comin' through this blanket. Unnerstan'? I only lettin' you live cause my bros want some good blowjobs. You owe me a pack of Luckies by the way.''

Three days later, Coon walked out the doors of the massive penitentiary, looked up at the bright sun, and smiled broadly. He breathed a deep breath of fresh air and strolled nonchalantly over to a shiny silver Cadillac stretch limo. A chauffeur bowed slightly as the ex-con climbed in the massive back and closed the door behind him.

Five months later, Coon stood in municipal court in Hamilton county, Ohio before a stern-faced judge. Next to Coon was a very high priced attorney with a very distinguished look and a kind face.

"But I do not understand why you would want to change your last name to Greenfield. That's Jewish and you're an African-American," the judge said.

The attorney responded, "If it please the court, your honor, my client chose . . ."

Coon interrupted, "Your honor, my attorney told you that I want to legally change my name because I am an ex-convict, and I am ready to completely turn my life around."

The judge, obviously touched by Coon's words so far, leaned forward in his massive leather chair as Coon continued his convincing speech. "Anyhow, your honor, I want to change my name to Robert Greenfield because that was the name of a nice Jewish man who owned a deli in my neighborhood growing up, and he was the only person who ever treated me good as a child."

The judge smiled warmly and said, "The petition for name change is granted . . . and good luck to you, young man."

Coon and his attorney both smiled and shook hands eagerly before leaving the courtroom.

In actuality, a brilliant jeweler named Reuben Greenfield had become a bitter enemy of James Earl Smith without even knowing it. The man had refused to personally make some expensive jewelry for Smith, because Smith wanted the man personally to make it instead of one of his employees. Smith was the kind of man who hated to lose, fanatically, but Reuben Greenfield never paid much attention to the incident.

Six months later, a scene was reenacted which had already put millions into the coffers of James Earl Smith. One of Smith's confidential employees bought a one-million-dollar sliding term life insurance policy on Reuben Greenfield. The beneficiary was Robert Greenfield, a name that certainly would not arouse any suspicion if spotted on a computer readout or client list. The policy was a double indemnity policy in the event of accidental death. Not long after that, naturally, Reuben Greenfield's car went off a bridge one rainy night.

Robert Greenfield, alias Coon, inherited two million dollars and got to keep ten percent of it, as he had agreed while still in the penitentiary when he had been approached with the scheme by one of Smith's crooked attorneys. He had two hundred thousand dollars to his name, and he was not greedy about Smith getting the remaining $1,800,000. He couldn't wait until he arrived at his new home in southern Mexico. In short, Coon was a happy camper.

The day finally came when Robert Greenfield was picked up by private plane at the rendezvous point outside Brownsville, Texas and was flown toward his new home south of the border. His plans were to spend the rest of his life snorting good blow, drinking, and getting laid in the sunshine.

James Earl Smith's plans for his new employee were somewhat different. He planned to bring Coon back up to the States to perform certain tasks from time to time. The only problem with the plan was that Natty Tracker shortened James Earl Smith's life considerably, and Smith had never had a chance to use Robert again. The short man did indeed get laid a lot, get stoned a lot, and get drunk a lot. He also got very broke. Therefore, he had returned to the States and immediately got a job. He was paid five thousand dollars up front with a promise of fifty thousand more when the job was finished to travel to Colorado Springs, Colorado and blow away a guy named Nathaniel Hawthorne Tracker. The man who hired him was another con Coon had known from the Ohio Pen named Drip Randolph. Drip was now called Derrick, his given name, and was a member of SAFE-PEACE. In fact, he was the secretary of the organization and was in direct contact with Reed Forest.

Dee Light had a body that was incredible. Her legs were long, lithe, and very muscular. Her hips were nicely rounded, as were her buttocks. The sun glistened on the sparse tangle of bright red pubic hair and beads of perspiration were starting to pop out on her flat muscular tummy. Above that were very firm, full breasts that still showed some whiteness from a bikini tan. A breeze came down off Cheyenne Mountain and created ripples across the surface of Natty's swimming pool. It also cooled the sweat-covered body of the tall lady and made her nipples harden and stand up erect like the nearby mountain peaks. Her very long, flaming red hair lay in all directions on the chaise lounge at poolside and framed a face that seemed to have been molded after several dreams about Venus.

The mighty Titan lay next to the pool at her side. Suddenly, the giant wolf/dog's ears pricked forward, and his nostrils flared rapidly. Somebody was approaching but was still out of sight. Dee was napping deeply and comfortably. Her gun was in her bag which was farther away from the pool, but Dee wasn't uncomfortable with that because Tracker had perfected his security system to the n-th degree. Even though he was in Washington for a meeting with Wally Rampart, the beautiful Presidential guard felt completely relaxed at Tracker's mansion. Dee could have gone with him, but she was vacationing and was happy to get away from Washington. She didn't know that the big wolf/dog at her side had silently disappeared to check out an intruder and had not returned.

A shadow crawled out from one corner of the house and moved silently along the ground to the corner of the pool by the diving board. It was a tall man, and he looked at the beautiful redhead napping by the pool. The man very slowly and silently slipped off his clothes, left them under the diving board, and slid quietly into the water.

Still sleeping soundly, Dee felt only the warmth of the sun and dreamed of Natty's return tomorrow. She shifted her body slightly as she dreamed of his touch and his lips on her.

The intruder took one more look at the sleeping beauty, took a deep breath, and whale-rolled into the water. He swam underwater, kicking powerfully, and in a few seconds, his head came silently out of the water at the pool's edge by the woman. He now got a closer look at her and couldn't believe her breathtaking beauty. The man easily pushed on the pool's edge with his hands and lifted his tremendously powerful body up out of the water. Standing up straight now, he looked down at her and his breathing quickened. He got an erection and wondered if she would scream if she opened her eyes now. He noticed the handbag and thought about getting shot. The man knew this was Dee Light and that she was a Secret Service agent. He didn't want to try to take her sexually and get shot in the process, but he knew he had to have this woman. He was literally throbbing with sexual desire for her; her beauty was just too overwhelming.

The man sneaked in his bare feet over to the handbag and moved it far out of her reach, being careful not to let his shadow fall across her face or any drips of water fall off him and blow onto her in the breeze. He dropped onto all fours and slowly, carefully crawled back over to the chaise lounge.

Dee still slept peacefully, and Titan was nowhere to be found. The man grabbed her towel, lying on a nearby table, and quietly dried his hair, shoulders, and face. He didn't want a wayward drip of water waking her before he was ready for her to be taken by him.

Now he stood on his knees at the side of the chaise and marveled at her body. He wondered where he should start and then his eyes fixed on the red triangle of pubic hair. The man smiled to himself. His head moved forward and down toward the red triangle. His lips parted, and he prepared himself for her to jump with fear when they went into his target. She smelled to him completely feminine, and his mouth found its mark.

Dee's whole body tensed, and she started to scream, and he pushed his face a little harder into that area. The Secret Service agent grabbed the man by the hair and pulled him into her even tighter.

"Oh, Natty," she purred, "you came home early. Ooh, Natty, you came, you came."

Tracker lifted his face and smiled at her. Her chest heaved in and out, and she looked at him wide-eyed and flushed.

He said, "Can't speak now."

He kissed her body again in the same way, and she started panting like a new puppy.

Between moans and excited whimpers, Dee asked, "Why?"

Impish grin on his face, he lifted his face again, smiled at her, and said, "Cat's got my tongue."

"Ooh, Tracker."

Two hours later, the couple had moved to Natty's massive bedroom but were still making love. They showered and slipped on their clothes when the doorbell rang.

Tracker looked at his television set and in a commanding voice said, "Monitor on."

The television set came on and Natty said, "Security, front door."

A split-screen image came on, and Natty saw a tall well-dressed, Latin-looking man in sunglasses and a solid blue suit. He had neatly cut black hair and a black moustache that came just to the edge of his lips. He wore a white shirt, neatly shined black shoes, and a maroon tie. He had a good build. Both camera angles revealed a bulge in the man's suit coat that Natty identified as a pistol.

Tracker said, "Communications, front door."

There were two beeps, and Natty said, "Yes, may I help you?"

The man queried, "Mr. Tracker?"

Natty said, "Titan, hold."

The man turned and saw the mighty wolf/dog directly behind him on the porch, and Titan promptly sat down, ears pricked forward, ready to launch himself at the slightest provocation.

Natty said, "Yes, I'm Tracker."

The man pulled a leather wallet out of his inside coat pocket and held it up in front of one of the cameras. It opened to show an FBI badge and an identification card.

The man said in a gravelly voice with a slight Spanish accent, "I am Special Agent Duncan Paez, Federal Bureau of Investigation. I was supposed to meet another agent here named Dominic Lombardi."

Natty said, "Yes, Mister Paez, he called me about it. Come in please and turn right. Have a seat in the living room. I'll be right down."

Then Natty said, "Mike off, unlock front door, monitor off."

Agent Paez heard the door unlock, and he reached out and twisted the handle on the right door of the twin oak doors. The man stepped into the foyer and whistled to himself as he looked around at the beautiful mansion. All of a sudden, the giant wolf/dog, which had been out front with him, appeared from the back of the house. Titan walked over and calmly lay down in front of the living

room fireplace, an easy step and a lunge to reach the possible intruder.

The now-nervous FBI agent patted his leg and said,
"C'mere, boy, C'mere."

The dog, its massive head lying across his front legs,
just looked at the intruder with a low growl emanating
from deep within his barrel chest.

"Steady," Tracker said as the agent snapped his head
and looked at the tall super-detective entering the room
accompanied by a beautiful redheaded woman.

Tracker sized up the good-looking Latino Fed and shook
hands with him, a smile on his face.

"Pleased to meet you," Natty said. "This is Ms. Dee
Light, my best friend."

Her beautiful eyes lit up with Natty's comment, and she
extended her hand and flashed a smile at the agent.

"Pleased to meet you, Miss Light," Duncan said.

There was a knock on the door, and the FBI agent was
surprised when he saw Natty look at the living room television set and say, "Monitor, on. Security, front door."

The set came on immediately with the split screen,
two-camera shot of the front door with Agent Dominic
Lombardi standing in front of it.

"Communications, front door," Natty said. "Dominic,
come in. Mike off, monitor off."

Dominic walked into Natty's massive living room and
was greeted by a warm hug from Tracker. Next, he was
introduced to Dee, and then he walked over to shake hands
with Duncan.

"How you doin'?" Dom said. "Dom Lombardi. Nice
to put a name to the face."

Duncan shook hands, smiled warmly, and said, "Hi,
how are you doing? Pleased to meet you," with a voice
that sounded like a steel bucket full of nuts and bolts being
dragged over a railroad bed.

Tracker said, "You mean you two don't know each
other?"

Dominic said, "No, Duncan got assigned to me, and I told him to meet me here."

Duncan said, "I just resigned my commission in the Army and transferred my retirement to the FBI."

This intrigued Natty, so he said, "Why would you resign your commission? What was your MOS?"

Paez smiled warmly, "Seven-thirteen-ninety-three, intelligence officer. The FBI was needing some people with my background and training, so I jumped at the chance to be an FBI agent. I guess I'm just a rookie now."

Natty said, "Did you go to jump school?"

Duncan laughed and said, "No way. Only two things fall from the sky: birdshit and airborne."

Dom said, "Well, you sure are welcome aboard. I've been assigned to the Reed Forest case. I worked it undercover for a while, but last week, my cover got blown and I almost got killed. If it wasn't for Mister Tracker here, I would be deader than hell right now."

"No kidding," Duncan said. "How did that happen?"

All four sat down and drank a couple of pots of coffee while Dom and Natty explained to Duncan and Dee the details of what had happened. Nobody could believe that Dom was already able to come back to work after having been buried alive, but he wouldn't let his boss take him off the case. Natty decided that he really liked Dom Lombardi and had a lot of respect for him, too.

Tracker took the two men to his computer center and showed them how to start accessing information with the computers. The three men agreed that they should first try to discover and locate any close friends and relatives Reed Forest might have. They decided to also look for known members of the SAFE-PEACE organization who might have a vacant house or farm in which Reed might be hiding.

After several hours, Natty announced that he had to go to the store to buy some groceries. Dom let him know that the two agents would accompany him since Reed still wanted him dead. Natty argued for a bit, but he knew these men had their orders and wouldn't listen to him. They agreed that Dom would ride with Natty in his car and Duncan would follow in his non-descript government car.

As they made the turn at the end of Natty's street, none of them saw a pair of eyes watching them. Coon Morgan was in a stolen Merc Cougar he had picked up at the parking lot at Denver's Stapleton International Airport. He carefully followed the two cars at a safe distance. His contact had given him a photograph of Tracker, and he was easy to spot as the driver of the customized jet-black 1969 Corvette Sting Ray with flared fenders. He could hear the rumbling of the 454-cubic-inch powermill as it took off from a stop sign and turned left onto Nevada Avenue. Traffic was heavy with off-duty Fourth Infantry Division soldiers from nearby Fort Carson.

The two cars, with the third following, weaved their way down Nevada toward downtown Colorado Springs and turned left into a grocery store parking lot caddy-corner from Southgate Center. Coon pulled in behind them and parked several rows away. He reached into the back of his car and grabbed hold of a bolt action .308 caliber rifle with an eight-power Redfield scope mounted on top. He sat and waited while the other three walked into the grocery store.

They emerged twenty minutes later with Natty pushing a cart with four bags of groceries. Coon rolled down his window and rested the rifle stock on the door frame. He put Tracker's head in the crosshairs and started to squeeze the trigger. A gun went off to his left a split-second before his, and something slammed his rifle to the right.

He looked at his left arm, saw blood, and suddenly felt pain. The rifle stock was shattered, and the scope was just then hitting the blacktop ten feet away. Instinctively, Coon clawed for the Berretta nine millimeter semi-automatic tucked into his waistband and flipped the safety off. He noticed that the three black-haired men were behind the Corvette and were firing at him now.

He realized then that he had been shot from the left, turned his attention that way, and saw a beautiful red-haired woman in a spread-legged stance, holding a big pistol with her right hand and steadying it with the left. His eyes opened wide as he decided to bring his pistol up and open fire on her. Everything seemed to be in slow motion as the beautiful white woman shook her head. He kept bringing his gun up, however, and before it cleared the window of the car, he saw two bright flashes of light shoot out of her gun, but he could only stare at the beauty of her face. He felt himself fly backward across the front seat of his car, and he felt the back of his head slam against the side window and crash through it. He briefly looked up at the blue cloudless sky and then slid back into the car. Coon looked down at the spreading crimson stains on his chest and saw blood oozing out of one hole on the right and spurting out of another on the left side of his upper chest. He wondered why it was there. He looked back at the beautiful woman and thought that he needed to shoot her, so he lifted his gun again. She was shaking her head again, and he felt something slam into his throat, heard a snap inside his neck, and then realized that he had seen her gun spout flames again. His head fell forward on his chest, and he saw blood everywhere and then decided that he wanted a nap. Coon thought about Badass Rivers, and he tried to laugh and say that he was nobody's bitch, but he couldn't speak or laugh, only think it. He smelled feces, wondered where it was coming from, and then saw that he had wet his pants in addition. He thought his mom would really be mad, and he closed his eyes to take his nap. He napped forever.

Dee Light respected the FBI, but she was Secret Service, and her job was protecting the lives of VIPs. That was what she had been trained for, so she had waited, knowing where Natty was going to go, and then discreetly followed. She had done this a number of times, always returning to the house a bit ahead of Natty. She didn't know that Tracker had often seen her tracks, felt the hood of her car, and smiled to himself about his lover/protector. Natty never really got angry about it. He appreciated her concern and that of the President, who he was sure encouraged such practices and frequent visits to Natty.

The gorgeous federal bodyguard walked forward, keeping close to cars she could dive behind for cover. A Colorado Springs cop roared into the parking lot and got out covering her with his pistol. Dee was holding her weapon out at arm's length, still in the double-handed grip. She yanked a badge out of her cleavage and it hung from a gold chain around her neck right in front of her ample bosom.

Not taking her eyes off the car, she hollered, "U.S. Secret Service! Point your fucking gun at the perp in that car, officer, not at me!"

The young cop nervously replied, "Yes, ma'am!"

Still moving toward Coon's car, she yelled again, "Stay back with your cruiser while I check it out!"

"Yes, ma'am." he yelled, and he kept his eyes glued on the Cougar for any sign of foul play.

Dee made it to Coon's car and ducked behind the trunk. She eased along the side with her gun at the ready, peeked in, gun pointing first, and ducked back. She looked again and this time held her position. Dee let out her breath and sighed. She opened the door with one hand, grabbed Coon's ankle, and felt for a pulse along the side of the ankle. There was none. A tear started to appear in the corner of her eye and she stopped it. She hadn't checked on Natty and the others or checked for more assassins.

Letting her gun arm hang down loosely, she realized she was drenched with sweat.

She now looked at the young Colorado Springs officer and yelled, "It's okay. This one's dead. Make sure there're no more hitmen around."

Dee ran toward the Corvette, but didn't see anyone

standing. Her heart pounded wildly in her chest and she choked back tears. She knew that Natty had to be hit or he would be backing her up. Rolling across the hood of the customized Mako Shark, she realized her worst fears as she shouted at the forming crowd to get back. Both FBI agents were trying to give Natty first aid as he lay on his back in a pool of blood. There was a big bullet exit wound high on his left side. Bright red blood bubbled out of the wound.

Tears rolling down her cheeks, she shoved the two agents back and grabbed his shirt and tore it open. A wheezing sound came out of the hole in his chest, and she tore the makeshift bandage off that Dom had placed there.

"Is there anything covered with plastic in the groceries?" she asked.

Duncan Paez shouted, "The grocery bags are plastic!"

"Give me two of them, he has a sucking chest wound," Dee commanded. "Dominic, run inside and grab some tape quickly!"

He took off while Paez dumped the groceries on the ground and handed her the bags. Onlookers had gathered, and police were pouring onto the scene now. One sergeant tried to take over from Dee, but she made him back off with a look and a shout. Someone said that an ambulance was on the way.

Still covering the entrance and exit wounds with the two plastic bags and making it airtight with the tape, Dee talked to the unconscious Tracker. "Natty Tracker, don't you die, you son of a bitch. I love you. Do you hear me?"

An ambulance arrived, and Dee told them what she had done in a very businesslike manner and then turned to Tracker and repeated her words. As the paramedics knelt over him, she saw a slight smile appear on his lips, and she started crying hysterically. She walked over to Dom, and he held her while she cried on his chest.

"You're Secret Service?" Duncan said.

Dee nodded her head and continued to cry. She finally

got hold of herself, walked over to the ambulance, and climbed on board as they placed Tracker inside on a gurney.

A Colorado Springs police lieutenant came over and said, "Ma'am, we've got to get your report."

"At the hospital," Dee said tersely.

"Yes, ma'am," he said, and the door to the ambulance was closed, and Tracker was rushed to the hospital.

Dee started to talk to Tracker but changed her mind, moving forward to the front of the ambulance where she commandeered the radio and started barking instructions about notifying the commanding general of NORAD and immediately calling the White House. Then Dee thought of something. She moved back to Tracker and leaned over him.

The paramedic working on him grabbed her gently by both upper arms, moved her back, and said, "I know you're concerned, miss, but we're trying to save his life."

Dee yanked her arms loose, pointed at her badge, and said, "I want you to. I won't get in your way, but this is a matter of national security."

She leaned over, felt around on Natty's neck until she found the sensor under his skin, and pushed on it. Wally Rampart was in his office and looked at the screen. Dee then opened one of Natty's eyelids and spoke at it while the two EMTs stared in disbelief.

"General, if you are listening, Natty has been shot, and we're on our way to Penrose Hospital in Colorado Springs. He's in very bad shape and is unconscious. The bullet was high power and hit him from behind and exited out the front. I know his lung was hit and maybe his heart. You have to do something." Dee stopped and started crying again.

She then turned the sensor off.

Dee tried to keep it together during the ride to the hospital but couldn't. She kept falling to pieces, and it really hit her how much she truly did love Natty Tracker. She not only loved him, but his comment about her being his best friend was really true. She did like him a lot. If Natty should die, she thought, part of her would die with him. Then a firm resolve took over. Part of what was upsetting her was the fact that Tracker always seemed so damned invincible.

He was the man she loved, and he was her best friend. She would have to be strong, tough, and alert for Natty. Somebody wanted Tracker very dead. Somebody who was a master of disguise and couldn't be seen. Somebody who was very smart, wealthy, and extremely ruthless. Somebody by the name of Reed Forest.

"Miss, miss," one of the paramedics said, "I don't believe this, but he just opened his eyes."

Dee wiped away her tears and hovered over Natty just as they pulled into the emergency entrance to the hospital. He barely managed a smile.

She said, "Natty, I love you, so you fight. Do you hear me?"

His eyes opened again, and he again smiled weakly.

His lips formed the words "Come here."

She leaned over all the way, and Natty just barely whispered, "Thirty-five alpha."

He passed out again, and his head fell to the side as the ambulance stopped. The doors were flung open, and several helicopters hovered noisely overhead. A team of doctors and nurses waited at the door, and Dee knew that she had gotten through to Wally Rampart. She identified herself as Secret Service and accompanied the gurney into the hospital.

The team rushed him immediately into surgery and tried to stop Dee from coming in.

She bulled her way past several people, and the head surgeon said, "I don't want you in here, young lady."

Dee said, "I'm Secret Service, and I'm trying to protect him."

The doctor said to somebody else, "Call security and have her removed."

He then looked at Dee and said, "I don't care if you're the President. I'm trying to save his life, and this is my operating room. Now get out."

Two hospital security officers burst in to the OR and rushed over to Dee.

The doctor said, "Remove her immediately."

One of the two guards grabbed the beautiful redhead. A half second later, he was on the floor screaming in pain from the wrist lock she put on him. Her right hand went into her purse and came out with a big gun. Dee's face was redder than her hair. She shoved the barrel of the gun into the nostril of the man she was joint-locking, and his eyes opened like a blimp hangar door.

Staring at the guards and cocking the pistol, Dee said, "Now, Doc, I work for the President of the United States, not you. I will stay out of the way, but I am not leaving here, so get your job done. Now, you two rent-a-cops get the fuck out of here before I get angry."

Both security guards made a very hasty retreat, and the surgeon shut his mouth as far as Dee went. Natty was prepped and they started working on him, after Dee was politely asked to put on a sterile gown and mask. They operated for six hours, and his heart stopped twice. Tears started to flow down Dee's cheeks each time, but she stopped them with her firm resolve.

Finally, Natty was taken to post-op. This time the surgeon didn't argue with Dee; he let her alone. When they wheeled Natty into post-op, however, Dee got a special surprise. The place was now swarming with Secret Service and FBI agents. Dee's supervisor had even flown in from D.C. to coordinate the security for Tracker. The surgeon then met with Dee, and they made up for their earlier confrontation. He had found out all the details and told her how she had saved Tracker's life by putting the airtight bandages on Natty's sucking chest wound.

Tracker was moved into intensive care, with guards everywhere. He slept deeply but he dreamt. He was a magnificent warrior of the Sioux tribe in the eighteen hundreds, but in the dream he had blood running down his chest, and a lance was sticking through his back and out the front of his ribcage. Thrown from his magnificent buckskin gelding, Eagle, Natty was lying on his back in a half-sitting position. Women, squaws actually, were crying and asking him not to die.

In the dream, instead of the Sioux word for God, he used the Apache word belying his other ancestral heritage, when he proudly responded, "I am He Who Tracks The Eagle and will not die. *Usen*, the Great Mystery, has called upon me to fight against those with no honor. He has told me to strike down those who would make war on the people of all my tribes."

Tracker's mother knelt in front of him. Tears in her eyes and jaw thrust out with pride, she wrapped her arms around him in an embrace. She leaned back and her face became Dee Light's. Tracker kissed her long and deep, and their faces came apart, and she was Doctor Fancy Bird. She took off her clothes and pulled her body close to him, they kissed again, and suddenly she turned into a white dove and flew away into the clouds. There was still a nude lover with him, however, under the buffalo robe and it was Dee Light.

All of a sudden, there were loud war whoops and the thundering of hooves, and the wounded brave tried to stand, but the pain was too great. Dee jumped out of the robe and had war paint on. It was the black racoon mask and red eagle talons of Tracker's face paint. She was bare-breasted but wore the loincloth of a male warrior. She looked mighty and fierce, yet beautiful at the same time. She had a bow in one hand, a war club in the other, and she ran to the buckskin horse and vaulted onto his back.

The beauty looked at Tracker and said, "You are my

man. You will rest and heal, and I will strike down our enemies.''

Dee gave out a whoop and kicked the line-back dun with her calves, and the sinewy horse launched itself at the charging warriors. He Who Tracks The Eagle leaned back and rested, a smile on his face, as he watched his lover go through the enemy warriors, clubbing braves off their ponies left and right. Feeling safe and secure, he fell asleep in the dream and slept peacefully wrapped in a warm buffalo robe.

Wally Rampart had flown in and was meeting with Dee Light and Special Agents Paez and Lombardi in Natty's computer center. She had gotten special permission from her supervisor to work on the case. Actually, it was to provide Tracker with security, but she rationalized it as the opportunity to try to find Reed Forest and eliminate him.

Wally said, ''Did Tracker say anything else to you?''

Dee said, ''No, but it had to be very important. Thirty-five alpha; I just can't figure it out.''

''We got this report in from an FBI interrogation of two of Forest's bodyguards,'' Wally said, handing copies of a fourteen-page document to the others. ''It seems that Reed Forest is a bisexual and had several male lovers, including his nextdoor neighbor, Eric Handover.''

''Bullshit,'' Duncan said laughing. ''You mean to tell me that Eric Handover, the football player, is gay, and Reed Forest, the lover boy I've seen in so many movies, is his boyfriend?''

While the others went through the report, Dee called the hospital. She got a sad look on her face, it seemed to Wally, and then she said something, hung up, and returned to the table.

''Any change?'' Dom asked.

''No, none at all,'' Dee said with resignation.

"Wait a minute," Wally said, staring at one of Tracker's computer screens. "Come here, look at this."

"Dee, do you know how to do a split-screen on this?" Wally continued.

"Sure," she replied, sitting down at the computer console. "What do you want?"

Wally was enthusiastic when he said, "Put the physical description of Reed Forest up there on one side and then take the description of Eric Handover from that list and put it next to it."

Dee did so and everyone stared at the screen as grins appeared on their faces. Eric weighed fifteen pounds more than Reed. Other than that, their physical descriptions were identical.

Wally picked up the phone and ordered his private jet to be ready at Petersen Air Force Base. Dom Lombardi picked up another phone and called his field supervisor. They packed up their briefcases while Paez pulled out his Ruger Redhawk stainless steel .44 Magnum and checked his bullets. He was using expanders.

All four stared out the door, and Dom winked at Duncan and said, "Hey, that's not a government-issued cannon or ammo, you know."

Duncan said, "Yeah, I know. I plan to stay alive."

Dee stopped at the door and said, "You go on to LA. I'm staying here with Natty."

They left, and Dee went to Tracker's room and threw herself across his bed and started crying. She let the racking sobs flow from her and let the floodgates open. She was worried about Tracker. She was also worried about Forest trying again, because he knew that Tracker, if he lived, would never rest until Reed was dead. The theory that Reed Forest had killed his lover made sense, but Dee had learned long before to never take anything for granted, especially in the business of being one of the world's premiere bodyguards. She would watch over Natty Tracker and take nothing lightly.

Dee was so worried after she returned to the mansion that she continued to cry and finally fell asleep on the bed. She awakened twenty minutes later with Titan lying next to her on the big bed. She wrapped her arm around his neck and gave him a big hug.

Holding and petting the big dog, Dee thought back to when she and Tracker met and then the first time they made love. He had been assigned to take out the Ryoku Rai Kyookai, the Green Lightning Society, a notorious Japanese mafia-like organization similar to the Yakuza. After taking care of some so-called ninjas out in the wilds of the Sangre de Cristo mountains, he had returned and took Dee to the newly opened Mirage Resort Hotel and casino in Las Vegas, Nevada.

Their first time making love had been rushed and hurried. The second time was slow and patient and wonderful. She recalled the last time at the Mirage.

Tracker looked out the window of his suite in the Mirage. Dee Light got out of the bed and walked over and wrapped her slender arm around his muscular waist and watched out the window with him. They saw cars and pedestrians moving up and down the dizzying street full of lights and neon signs which was named Las Vegas Boulevard but called "the Strip" by locals and tourists alike. Between them and the Strip stood beautiful jungle trees and palms, gorgeous pools with cascading falls, and a dome-shaped manmade mini-volcano. Water erupted from the dome as red and orange lights shined upward from underneath.

Tracker turned and kissed Dee while the red and orange lights played on the sides of their faces. His fingers traced little trails all over her smooth skin. She shivered as his fingers started at her buttocks and ran lightly up her spine. She felt his excitement pushing against her, and she breathed in short excited breaths. Natty had not been with a woman who could excite him so much and so often in a very long time.

Dee was a class act. A patent and copyright attorney, or so he thought at the time, she was intelligent, independent, and charming. She was also strong enough to allow Natty to feel like he was in charge and protective of her.

The backs of his fingers ran lightly, very lightly, up over her shoulders and along her neck under her ears. She took a deep breath and started bending at her knees with her lips sliding down his copper torso. Then Tracker's beeper went off.

He walked over to the nightstand and looked at the number on the digital pager. He was to call his answering machine. He called and received the message from CIA headquarters. Half an hour later, Natty and Dee were in a white stretch limo on their way to Nellis Air Force Base where his Lear jet was safely hangered under guard. Natty refueled at Burbank Airport and again at Honolulu where he left Dee, against her protests, at a fancy resort hotel. He went on to Tokyo and eventually wiped out the whole organization.

She thought about their adventures together and how important their work was to their lives. On the other hand, with Natty lying near death's door in the hospital, Dee realized that she would give up her career in a New York minute to marry him and bear his children, if Tracker asked her.

She dropped to her knees next to the bed, entwined her fingers, and prayed like she had never prayed before.

One half hour later, after forcing herself to eat a sandwich, Dee left Natty's mansion driving his black Mako Shark 'Vette. The monstrous wolf/dog sat next to her as she drove to the hospital. Dee had to do some forceful speaking at the hospital and show her badge around to get the dog to the private, closely guarded, makeshift ICU unit Tracker was in.

Titan was allowed to stay in Tracker's room as additional security. He immediately jumped up with his forepaws on the bed and licked Natty's face. A smile appeared, and Dee called the nurses over.

Within five minutes, Natty was awake, but just barely. After the nurses checked his vitals and the doctor checked him over, Dee went to the side of the bed and leaned over, stroking his forehead. She slipped something under his pillow and whispered in his ear. Natty reached up under the pillow and smiled at her.

He whispered, "I love you, Dee," and passed out again.

Natty awakened two other times that night, and Dee and Titan refused to leave his side. He couldn't talk, but Dee knew that he would live.

After midnight, Dee took a call from Wally Rampart and told him the good news about Natty's awakening. He told her that they couldn't find Eric Handover at his home next to Forest's. Duncan Paez had remained outside on the grounds and caught Handover coming out of a hidden tunnel in the yard which ran to Forest's poolhouse. The retired football player had apparently panicked and pulled a twenty-five automatic pistol, and Duncan blew most of his head off with his .44 Magnum. They had checked carefully and were having more tests run, but apparently Eric Handover was who he purported to be. He had died for nothing. Wally said that it was the first time Paez had shot a man and the agent was upset about it. All three were heading back quickly, though, since Natty was obviously still very much in danger.

They arrived at the hospital a little after noon the next day. Wally convinced the ICU nurse to let them all come to Natty's bedside. Tracker's eyes opened and he smiled.

Looking at the old general, Tracker said, "Fuck you, don't say it."

Wally started laughing and the rest followed suit. Paez was clearly upset by what had happened in Beverly Hills. Natty acted sympathetic.

Tracker said, "You ever see Reed Forest's anti-Vietnam war movie called *Orange in the Green*?"

"No, I didn't," Duncan replied sadly. "Why?"

Tracker said weakly, "Oh, he's just such a great actor. I read he really goes overboard researching his roles."

Now, Dee, Wally, Dom, and Duncan all wondered what the hell he was getting at as his voice strained to get the words out.

Tracker continued, "The movie was about an intelligence officer with the One Hundred First Airborne Division in Vietnam. He discovered some records showing that the defoliant Agent Orange was indeed toxic, but some Army brass were going to cover it up. They tried to kill Reed's character in the process."

Duncan Paez started to fidget, and Natty continued, "Reed's character had an MOS of seven-thirteen-ninety-three. The thirteen-ninety-three meant intelligence officer, but the seven prefix meant airborne-qualified. You told me that you were not airborne, but you said your MOS was seven-thirteen-ninety-three. Some years ago, by the way, the Army changed its old MOS designation system. For some time now, the MOS for a general intelligence officer has been thirty-five alpha. You hired that Robert Greenfield to come after me and shot me during the fight from behind. Why don't you lose the gravelly voice and accent and wipe off that dark pancake makeup, Reed? Hey, could I have your autograph?"

Titan launched himself from his prone position on the floor and streaked through the air as the big Ruger Redhawk started to come out of Reed Forest's shoulder holster. He missed the arm but his body slammed Reed against the wall. It was what Natty needed because he had miscalculated and didn't realize how much his wounds and weakened condition had slowed him. Nevertheless, his right hand shot out from under his pillow with one of his Glock 19 nine-millimeter semi-automatics in his hand. He squeezed five shots within one second, and they could all have been covered by a sliver dollar. The left breast pocket of Reed Forest's white shirt was completely ruined by the five bullets as they passed through it. Nobody else in the room had even had time to draw his weapon when they all saw Reed Forest slam against the wall and slide into a sitting position, lifeless eyes staring straight ahead. An unglamorous conclusion to his final performance, and with him died the dreams of SAFE-PEACE.

Dee ran over and threw her arms around Natty and they kissed. Titan jumped up on the bed with his front feet and licked his master's face while he was kissing Dee. Everyone in the room, including all the Secret Service agents who had rushed in, laughed at the sight.

Natty Tracker looked out the window at the clouds in the blue Colorado sky and pictured a white dove flying far away. He turned his attention back to his best friend and looked into her eyes. He saw two things: one was love and the other was his future.

IN A WORLD ENSLAVED,
THEY'RE FIGHTING BACK!

Freedom is dead in the year 2030—megacorporations rule with a silicon fist, and the once-proud people of the United States are now little more than citizen-slaves. Only one group of men and women can restore freedom and give America back to the people:

THE NIGHT WHISTLERS

The second American Revolution
is about to begin.

THE NIGHT WHISTLERS #1: by Dan Trevor
Available now from Jove Books!

Following is an exclusive preview . . .

Prologue

Los Angeles, 2030: Seen from afar, the skyline is not
all that different from the way it was in earlier decades.
True, the Wilshire corridor is stacked with tall buildings,
and there are new forms in the downtown complex: the
Mitsubishi Towers, a monstrous obelisk in black obsidian;
the Bank of Hamburg Center, suggesting a vaguely gothic
monolith; the Nippon Plaza with its ''Oriental Only'' dining room slowly revolving beneath hanging gardens; and,
peaking above them all like a needle in the sky, the Trans
Global Towers, housing the LAPD and their masters, Trans
Global Security Systems, a publicly held corporation.

The most noticeable difference in this city is a silver
serpentine arch snaking from downtown to Dodger Sta-
dium and into the Valley, and in other directions—to Santa
Monica, to San Bernardino, and to cities in the south. Yes,
at long last, the monorail was constructed. The original
underground Metro was abandoned soon after completion,
the hierarchy claiming it earthquake prone, the historians
claiming the power elite did not want an underground system of tunnels where people could not be seen, particularly since the subways in New York and other eastern
cities became hotbeds of resistance for a short period.

But to fully grasp the quality of life in this era, to really understand what it is like to live under the Corporate shadow, one ultimately has to step down from the towers and other heights. One has to go to the streets and join the rank and file.

Those not lucky enough to inherit executive positions usually live in company housing complexes—which are little more than tenements, depending upon the area. The quality of these establishments vary, generally determined by one's position on the Corporate ladder. All in all, however, they are grim—pitifully small, with thin walls and cheap appliances and furnishings. There are invariably, however, built-in televisions, most of them featuring seventy-two-inch screens and "Sensound." It is mandatory to view them during certain hours.

When not spouting propaganda, television is filled with mindless entertainment programming and endless streams of commercials exhorting the populace to "Buy! Buy! Buy!" For above all, this is a nation of consumers. Almost all products, poorly made and disposable, have built-in obsolescence. New Lines are frequently introduced as "better" and "improved," even though the changes are generally useless and cosmetic. Waste disposal has therefore become one of the major problems and industries of this society. A certain amount of one's Corporate wages is expected to be spent on consumer goods. This is monitored by the Internal Revenue Service and used somewhat as a test of loyalty, an indicator of an individual's willingness to contribute to society.

The Corporations take care of their own on other levels as well. Employees are, of course, offered incentive bonuses, although these are eaten quickly by increased taxes. They are also supplied with recreational facilities, health care, and a host of psychiatric programs, including Corporate-sponsored mood drugs. In truth, however, the psychiatric programs are more feared than welcomed, for psychiatry has long given up the twentieth century pretense that it possessed any kind of workable technology to enlighten individuals. Instead, it baldly admits its purpose to bring about "adjustment"—the control and subjugation of individuals "who don't fit in."

Because this is essentially a postindustrial age, and most of the heavy industry has long been shifted abroad to what was once called the Third World, the majority of jobs are basically clerical. There are entire armies of pale-faced word processors, battalions of managers, and legions of attorneys. Entire city blocks are dedicated to data entry facilities, and on any given night, literally thousands of soft-white monitors can be seen glowing through the glass.

There are also, of course, still a few smaller concerns: tawdry bars, gambling dens, cheap hotels, independent though licensed brothels, and the odd shop filled with all the dusty junk that only the poor will buy. And, naturally, there has always been menial labor. Finally there are the elderly and the unemployed, all of whom live in little more than slums.

Although ostensibly anyone may rise through the ranks to an executive position, it is not that simple. As set up, the system invites corruption. Even those who manage to pass the extremely stringent entrance exams and psychiatric tests find it virtually impossible to move up without a final qualifying factor: a sponsor. Unless one is fortunate enough to have friends or relatives in high places, one might as well not even try. If there ever was a classed society, this is it.

In a sense then, the world of 2030 is almost medieval. The Consortium chief executive officers in all the major once-industrial nations rule their regions with as much authority as any feudal lord, and the hordes of clerks are as tied to their keyboards as any serf was ever tied to the land. What were once mounted knights are now Corporate security officers. What was once the omnipotent church is now the psychiatric establishment.

But lest anyone say there is no hope of salvation from

this drudgery and entrapment, there are the national lotteries.

Corporately licensed and managed, the Great American Lottery is virtually a national passion. The multitude of ever-changing games are played with all the intensity and fervor of a life-and-death struggle, drawing more than one hundred million participants twice a week. There are systems of play that are as complex and arcane as any cabalistic theorem, and the selection of numbers has been elevated to a religious experience. Not that anyone ever seems to win. At least, not anyone that anyone knows. But at least there is still the dream of complete financial independence and relative freedom.

But if it is an impossible dream that keeps the populace alive, it is a nightmare that keeps them in line. Ever since the Great Upheaval, the Los Angeles Corporate Authority, and its enforcement arm, the LAPD (a Corporate division) have kept this city in an iron grip. And although the LAPD motto is still "To Protect and Service," its master has changed and its methods are as brutal as those of any secret police. It is much the same in all cities, with all enforcement agencies around the world under the authority of Trans Global.

What with little or no legal restraint, suspects are routinely executed on the streets, or taken to the interrogation centers and tortured to or past the brink of insanity. Corporate spies are everywhere. Dissent is not tolerated.

And yet, in spite of the apparently feudal structure, it must be remembered that this is a high-tech world, one of laser-enhanced surveillance vehicles, sensitive listening devices, spectral imaging weapon systems, ultrasonic crowd control instruments, and voice-activated firing mechanisms.

Thus, even if one were inclined to create a little havoc with, for instance, a late-twentieth-century assault rifle, the disparity is simply too great. Yes, the Uzi may once have been a formidable weapon, but it is nothing compared to a Panasonic mini-missile rounding the corner to hone in on your pounding heartbeat.

Still, despite the suppression, despite the enormous disparity of firepower, despite of the odds, there are still a few—literally a handful—who are compelled to resist. This savage world of financial totalitarianism has not subdued them. Rather, if it has taught them anything at all, it is that freedom can only be bought with will and courage and blood.

This is the lesson they are trying to bring to the American people, this and an ancient dream that has always stirred the hearts of men.

The dream of freedom.

1.

THE CITY WAS still sleeping when the whistling began. The streets were still deserted, and the night winds still rattled through strewn garbage. Now and again, from deep within the tenement bowels came reverberations of harsh shouts, the slamming of a loosely hinged door. But otherwise there was nothing beyond the echo of that solitary whistler.

For a full thirty seconds Phillip Wimple stood stock-still and listened, the collar of his sad and shapeless raincoat turned up against the foul wind. He looked out at the city with calm brown eyes, his slightly lined face expressionless. He stood as detectives the world over stand, with all the weight on his heels, hands jammed into the pockets of his trousers, his cropped, gray head slightly cocked to the left.

Although not a particularly reflective man, those high nocturnal melodies had always left Wimple vaguely pensive. As to the fragment of some half-remembered tune that continually tugs at one's memory, he had always felt compelled to listen—to turn his tired eyes to the grimy Los Angeles skyline and allow the sounds to enter him.

A patrolman approached a sleek doberman of a man in

Hitachi body armor and a Remco mini-gun harness. Below, on a stretch of filthy pavement that skirted the weed-grown hill, stood four more uniformed patrolmen. Gillette M-90s rested on their hips. The darkened visors of crash helmets concealed their eyes. Turbo-charged Marauders idled softly beside them in the blackness.

"With all due respect, sir, the Chief Inspector wants to know what's holding us up."

Wimple turned again, shifting his gaze to the distant outline of an angular face behind a smoked Marauder windshield. "Well, tell her that if she would be so kind as to join me on this vantage point, I would be more than happy to explain the delay."

"Sir?"

"Ask Miss Strom to come up here."

Wimple returned his gaze to the skyline. Although the whistling had grown fainter, scattered by the predawn breeze, the melody was still audible: high and cold above the city's haze; dark and threatening in the pit of his stomach.

The woman entered his field of vision, an undeniably grim figure in black spandex and vinyl boots—a full-figured woman, about an inch taller than his five-ten. Her shimmering windbreaker was emblazoned with the Corporate logo: twin lightning bolts enclosed in a fist. When Wimple had first laid on eyes on her, he took her as a welcome change from the usual Corporate overlord. Not only was she smart, but she was beautiful . . . in a carnivorous way. He had also liked her fire, her determination, and her willingess to fight for a budget. But that was three days ago. Now, watching her stiffly approach through the smog-choked weeds and yellowed litter, he realized that Miss Erica Strom was no different from any of the boardroom commandants sent down to ensure that the Los Angeles Police Department toed the Corporate line.

"You want to tell me what's going on?" Miss Strom planted herself beside him.

Wimple shrugged, studying her profile: the chiseled features, the red-slashed lips, the hair like a black lacquered helmet. "Ever heard a rattler's hiss?" he asked.

Strom narrowed her sea-green eyes at him. "What are you talking about?"

Wimple extended his finger to the sky to indicate the echo of the unseen whistlers. "That," he said. "That sound."

Withdrawing a smokeless cigarette, one of the Surgeon General–sanctioned brands that tasted like wet hay, Wimple said, "Think of it like this. We're the cavalry. They're the Indians. Maybe they can't touch us up here, but down there it's a whole different story."

"So what are you trying to tell me? That you want to call this patrol off? You want to turn around and go to bed, because some Devo starts whistling in the dark?" Her deep voice had a masculine edge, a hardness.

Wimple shook his head with a tired smirk. Devo: Corporate catchword for any socially deviate individual, generally from the menial work force. "No, Miss Strom," he said, "I'm not trying to tell you that I want to call the patrol off. I'm just saying that if we go down there now, we could find ourselves in one hell of a shit storm."

Strom returned the detective's smirk. "Is that so?"

"Yes, ma'am."

"Well, in that case, Detective, move your men on down. I can hardly wait."

Long favored by patrolmen throughout the Greater Los Angeles sprawl, the Nissan-Pontiac Marauder was a formidable machine. With a nine-liter, methane-charged power plant, the vehicle was capable of running down virtually anything on the road, and was virtually unstoppable by anything less than an armor-piercing shell. Long and low, it was not, however, built for comfort, and the off-road shocks always wreaked havoc on Wimple's spine.

He rode shotgun beside Miss Strom: shoulders hard

against the polymer seats, feet braced on the floorboards, right hand firm on the sissy bar. Earlier, when Strom had given the order to move out, there had been several whispered complaints from the patrolmen. Now, however, as the three-vehicle convoy descended into the black heart of the city, the radios were silent.

"Why don't you tell me about them?" Miss Strom said, easing the Marauder onto the wastes of First Street.

Wimple shrugged, his eyes scanning the tenement windows above. "There's not really much to tell," he replied. "About eighteen months ago, we start getting reports of a little Devo action from the outlying precincts. Vandalism mostly. Petty stuff. Then come July and one of the IRS stations goes up in smoke. After that, we start finding it spray-painted all over the walls: Night Whistlers."

"Any idea who's behind it?"

"Yeah, we've got some ideas."

Strom's thin lips hardened. "So what's been the problem? Why haven't you cleaned them out yet?"

Wimple lifted his gaze to the long blocks of tenements ahead—to the smashed windows and rotting doorways, the grimy, crumbling brickwork and trashed streets. "Well, let's just say that the Whistlers turned out to be a little more organized than we thought." His voice was dull, noncommittal. She gave him a quick look then went back to scanning the street.

They had entered the lower reaches of Ninth Street, and another long canyon of smog-browned tenements. For the most part, the residents here were members of the semi-skilled labor force, popularly known as the Menials, officially referred to in ethnological surveys as the Lower Middle Class. Included among their ranks were whole armies of word processors, retail clerks, delivery boys, receptionists, and secretaries. By and large, their lives were measured out in pitiful production bonuses, worthless stock options, and department store clearance sales. They also, of course, spent a lot time pouring over their lottery tickets, even more in front of their television screens, watching tedious Corporate-controlled programming. Still, no matter how blatant the propaganda, it was more entertaining than their dull existences.

The radio came alive with a harsh metallic burst from the last Marauder in the line: "Possible six-twenty on Hill."

Six-twenty meant curfew violation—which invariably meant Devo action.

Strom dropped her left hand from the steering wheel and activated the dispatch button on the dashboard. "Let's show them a response now, gentlemen." Then bringing the Marauder into a tight turn, she activated the spectral-imaging screen and switched the infrared cameras to the scan mode.

Wimple, however, preferred to use his eyes. He initially saw only a half-glimpsed vision among the heaps of uncollected refuse: a thin, brown figure in a drab-green duffle coat. For a moment, a single perverse moment, he actually considered saying nothing. He actually considered returning his gaze to the bleak stretch of road ahead, casually withdrawing another smokeless cigarette and keeping his mouth firmly shut. But even as this thought passed through his mind, the image of the fleeing figure appeared on the screen.

The radio crackled to life again with a voice from the second Marauder. "I've got clean visual."

There was a quick glimpse of a sprinting form beneath a sagging balcony, the sudden clamor of a trash can on the pavement.

Strom powered her vehicle into another hard turn, screeching full-throttle into the adjoining alley. Then, as she deftly lowered her thumb to activate the spotlight, he was suddenly there: a wiry Hispanic huddled beneath an ancient fire escape.

Strom activated the megaphone, and her voice boomed

out in harsh, clipped syllables: "Remain where you are! Any attempt to flee will be met with force!"

The figure stumbled back to the alley wall, glaring around like a blinded bull. He was younger than Wimple had first imagined, no more than ten or twelve. His duffle coat was army surplus. His blue jeans were Levi knock-offs. He also wore a pair of black market running shoes—the badge of the Devos.

Strom eased the Marauder to a stop alongside the number two and three vehicles. Then, reaching for the stun gun beneath the dash, she slipped free of her harness and turned to Wimple. "Come on, Detective, let me show you what law and order is all about."

Strom and Wimple approached the suspect slowly. To their left and right, scanning the rooftops with Nikon-Dow Night Vision Systems atop their M-90s, were the four helmeted patrolmen from the backup Marauders. Given the word, they would have been able to pour out some six hundred fragmentation flechettes in less than a fifty-second burst—more than enough to shred the kneeling suspect to a bloody pulp.

Wimple looked at the boy's scared eyes. They kept returning to the stun-gun that dangled from Strom's gloved hand.

Manufactured for Trans Global by Krause-Nova Electronics in Orange County, the XR50 Stun gun had become the last word on hand-held crowd control. It was capable of dispersing a scatter charge of nearly fifty-thousand volts, instantly immobilizing a two-hundred-pound man. At closer range, and against bare skin, the pain was beyond description.

The boy could not keep himself from shivering when Strom laid the cold tip of the stun gun against his cheek, could not keep himself from mouthing a silent plea. In response, however, Strom merely smiled, and turned to Wimple again.

"Why don't you see what he's carrying, Detective? Hmm? See what our little lost lamb has in his pockets."

Wimple pressed the boy facedown to the pavement, consciously avoiding the terrified eyes. He then lowered himself to a knee and mechanically began the search. On the first pass, he withdrew only a greasy deck of playing cards, a half-eaten chocolate bar, and a stainless steel identity tag made out to one Julio Cadiz. Then, almost regretfully, he slowly peeled a six-inch steak knife from the boy's left ankle.

"Well, well, well." Strom smiled. "What have we here?"

Wimple rose to his feet, turning the steak knife over in his fingers. "These things don't necessarily mean much."

Strom let her smile sag into another smirk. "Is that so, Detective?"

"It's just kind of a status symbol with these kids. They don't ever really use them. They just like to carry them around to show off to their buddies."

But by this point, Strom had already withdrawn a pair of keyless handcuffs . . . had already released the safety on the stun-gun.

She secured the boy's wrists behind his back, then yanked up his coat and T-shirt to expose the base of the spine. Although once or twice the boy emitted a pleading whimper, he still hadn't actually spoken.

"Tell your men to secure the area," Strom said as she hunkered down on the pavement beside the handcuffed boy. Then again when Wimple failed to respond: "Secure the area, Detective. Tell your men."

Wimple glanced over his shoulder to the blank faces of the patrolmen. Before he actually gave the order, however, he turned to the woman again. "Look, I'm not trying to tell you how to do your job, Miss Strom, but this is not going to get us anywhere. You understand what I'm saying? And this is not a safe place for us to be wasting our time."

Strom ran a contemplative hand along the gleaming shaft of the stun-gun, then dropped her gaze to the shivering boy. Not looking at Wimple, she finally said, "Detective, I think you should get your men to secure the area before this little brat starts screaming and brings out the whole neighborhood."

She waited until the patrolmen posted on the corner fixed their night vision systems on the balconies and roof-tops and chambered clips of flechettes into their weapons. Then very gently, very slowly, she pressed the cold tip of the stun gun to the boy's naked spine.

"Look—," Wimple began.

"Shut up, Detective," she said, her eyes cold, then lowered her gaze back to the boy.

"Well, now, young man. You and I are going to have a little heart to heart. You understand? A frank exchange of views, with you starting first."

An involuntary shudder crossed the thin, feral face of the boy. "Look, lady, I don't know—"

She clamped her hand to his mouth. "No, no, no. That's not how this game is played, my little friend. In this game, you don't speak until I ask a question. Got it?"

The boy may have tried to nod, but Strom had taken hold of his hair. Then, yanking back his head so that his ear was only inches from her lips, she whispered, "Whis-tlers, my little man. How about telling me what you know about the Whistlers?"

The boy responded with another frenzied shiver, then possibly attempted to mouth some sort of response. But by this time Strom had released his head, activated the stun gun, and pressed the tip home.

The boy seemed to react in definite stages to the volt-age, first arching up like a quivering fish, then growing wide-eyed and rigid as the scream tore out of his body. And even when it stopped, he still seemed to have diffi-culty breathing, while the left leg continued to tremble.

"Now, let's try it again, shall we?" Strom cooed. "Who . . . are . . . the Whistlers?"

The boy shook his head before answering in spluttering gasps. "Look, lady, I don't know what you're talking about. I swear to God. The Whistlers, that's just something that they write on the walls."

"Who writes it on the walls?"

"I don't know. Just some of the Devos around here. I don't know who they are."

"Just some of the Devos, huh? Well, I'm sorry, young man, but that's just not good enough." And lifting up his T-shirt again to expose the base of his spine, she laid down another fifty-thousand volts.

There was something horrifying about the way the boy's eyes grew impossibly wide as he thrashed on the pavement with another trailing scream. There was also something chilling about the way Strom's lips twisted up in a smile as she watched.

Wimple turned his head away, stared for a moment into some distant blackness. Finally, unable to stand the sobs any longer, he approached again.

"Look, don't you think that's enough, Miss Strom? *Miss Strom!*"

She slowly turned on her haunches to face him, her left hand still toying with the boy's sweat-drenched hair. "You got a problem, Detective?"

Wimple met her gaze for a full three seconds before answering, a full three seconds to taste the woman's hatred. "Yeah," he finally nodded. "I got a problem. Quite apart from my personal objection to this activity, I'd like to point out that you are seriously endangering my men. If you think that this neighborhood is asleep right now, you are sadly mistaken. The people up in those buildings know exactly what's going on down here. They know exactly what you're doing, and I can assure you that they don't like it."

She withdrew her fingers from the boy's hair, and his

head lolled back to the vomit-smeared pavement. "Well, now, that's very interesting, Detective. Because, you see, I *want* them to know what's going on here. I *want* them to hear every decibel of this little bastard's scream and, remember it—"

"Shut up!"

"How dare you tell me to—"

"Shut up and listen!" Wimple said, as the first cold notes of the solitary whistler wafted down from the blackened rooftops.